TWO NOVELLAS

Dead for the Last Time

Trouble in the Labor Camp

Books by John D. Nesbitt

For the Norden Boys
Lonesome Range
Black Hat Butte
Red Wind Crossing
Rancho Alegre
Raven Springs
Coyote Trail
Black Diamond Rendezvous
Man from Wolf River
Not a Rustler
West of Rock River
North of Cheyenne
Poacher's Moon
Adventures of the Ramrod Rider
A Good Man to Have in Camp
Keep the Wind in Your Face
Shadows on the Plain
Field Work
Blue Horse Mesa: Western Stories
Antelope Sky: Stories of the Modern West
Seasons in the Fields: Stories of a Golden West

Two Novellas:
"Dead for the Last Time"
"Trouble in the Labor Camp"

TWO NOVELLAS

Dead for the Last Time

Trouble in the Labor Camp

John D. Nesbitt

SPEAKING VOLUMES, LLC
NAPLES, FLORIDA
2016

TWO NOVELLAS
Dead for the Last Time
Trouble in the Labor Camp

These two novellas are works of fiction. Any resemblance of the characters herein to real persons, living or dead, is coincidental.

ISBN 978-1-62815-479-5

for my old pal Dave Madden

Table of Contents

Dead for the Last Time

Chapter One

I didn't know anyone was dead, much less killed, until after I had gone to the police station. When I was lingering in there I saw Jesse Bonner and Darnell Preston, which did not surprise me, as they were subject to being hauled in on any day of the week. On this day, they were sitting in two hard old oak chairs with straight backs and no arm rests, just slouched with their hands in front of them as they stared at the floor. I gave them a toss of the head and a half-smile, but all they gave me back was a hangdog look that I took to mean they had their ass in a sling. Later on I found out why they'd been hauled in and left to sit in those hard chairs where they couldn't even have a cigarette.

Meanwhile, I had business of my own to tend to with these cops. In a small town, you get your fun where you can find it, and I found mine, or the first part of it, in the laundromat. I had been sitting there, reading an article about Castro and Cuba in *Look* magazine and waiting for my clothes to run the last few minutes in the dryer, when a little girl had an incident with the soda pop machine. As she pulled out a bottle of orange soda, something in the machine went wrong and started coughing out a stream of nickels, one by one. Click, click, click, click, and so on. I went over and scraped the coins out of the dish and counted them. Forty-one, for a total of $2.05, which wasn't very much but more than an hour's wages, even if I had a job. The little girl claimed ten cents, the change she had coming from the quarter she had dropped into the slot to begin with, so now I had $1.95 of new money.

I bagged up my laundry in the pillow case I used for that purpose, and I set out on foot. It was the latter part of June, so the days were getting hot. I trudged for about a mile north on the highway until I came to Shady Grove, a little cabin and trailer court set down off the highway in an old stand of oak trees. I went to my trailer, which had been described to me as a fifteen-footer, and flopped down in front of the swamp cooler. Shortly after I moved in, I came to understand that the fifteen feet included the tongue length, so my living space was about twelve by eight. The cooler took up a fair amount of that space, but I was glad to have it.

As I lay there, I got to thinking about the money I had picked up at the laundromat. The girl's mother and some other old bird had seen me take it, and either of them might tell the owner. As a general rule, money in coin returns is finders-keepers, but I figured thirty-nine nickels probably went past the rule. Furthermore, if either of those other two people didn't like the looks of my long hair, or if they were a little jealous that someone else got the windfall, or a little of both, the local police would be all too willing to look me up. I didn't see any fun in that.

I did see the opportunity for a joke, though, and at the same time I could make the point that not all young folks with long hair were scurrilous hippies. So I decided to walk back into town and turn in the $1.95 to the local police.

3

At the city hall building, I went up the stairs and through an oak door with opaque glass, into the police department itself. That was when I first saw Jesse and Darnell. I tossed them a glance and turned to talk to two cops behind the counter. I must say I caught them unprepared. After a little uncertainty on their part, one of them ushered me into an inner office and gave me to a cloudy-faced fellow named Arnold, who took my statement and had me sign it. Then he typed me a receipt, in the old hunt-and-peck method on a crash-and-bang typewriter.

> *Recieved from Larry Sterne $1.95 in Change. Money came from the Pop Machine at the self Service laundry 5th and Tehama.*
> *R.L. Arnold #52 W.F.P.D.*

He signed it and gave it to me. As I admired his spelling and capitalization, I decided his receipt was a gem worth keeping.

When I walked out of the office into the waiting area, I saw Bonner and Preston still sitting there looking glum. I could feel the contrast. Here I was with a bounce in my step after watching Officer Arnold go through all of his labor, and here were these two would-be hoodlums, half-assed pals of mine, looking as if they'd been caught with a gas can and a coil of hose in their trunk. Or worse.

Back out on the street, I thought there would be no harm in walking past the laundromat, so I went that way. As I glanced in the window, I saw a lean guy about forty with slicked-back hair sweeping the floor. I went in and asked him if he was the owner. He said he was the manager. I told him about the nickels and how I had looked out for their safe-keeping. He thanked me. Then he offered to buy me a soda, which I declined. I was just about to leave when he asked if I'd heard what happened at the old milk factory.

"No, I didn't."

"Well, they found a dead man there."

"Really. Who was it?"

The manager lowered his voice and glanced toward the window and open door. "It was that old man Earle."

It registered real fast. He meant Clarence Earle, the old pervert who, as I heard it, used to lure boys into the abandoned factory and give them four bits to watch him expose himself and more. I had heard it from a couple of different sources, including Jesse Bonner and Darnell Preston. In one version of the story, Darnell said he had touched the old man's peter, and then he said he didn't. I never asked for clarification.

The manager spoke again, kind of confidential-like. "They just found him earlier in the day, and they've already brought in a couple of kids for questioning. Boys he took in there when they were a little younger, I guess."

I nodded. The whole idea was getting disagreeable. "Well," I said, "it sounds as if someone's going to be in trouble."

The man stood with the broomstick against his shoulder as he lit a cigarette. "Oh, yeah. Big trouble. Even if he *was* an old queer."

I walked back to my trailer, still in the heat of the afternoon, and was glad to see the shade of the oak trees covering
my little hut. I went in and turned on the cooler, and as I
loafed on the fold-down bed, I couldn't get the creepy news
out of my mind.

The old milk factory had been shut down for about four
years. It was a row of connected buildings, concrete and corrugated metal, all a dull grey and easy to ignore. It lay along
the west side of the railroad tracks, set back from the highway
that ran past it on that side. Other businesses were strung
along the tracks as well—a lumber yard, a feed store, and an
almond processing plant as the tracks went south; then going
north, an orange-packing co-op next to an olive plant with a
yard full of huge wooden vats, where rats came out after dark.
The milk factory was the biggest enterprise, and when it shut
down, the town lost its noon whistle as well as quite a few
decent-paying jobs. But when it was gone it was gone, and
the buildings didn't look much different from any old set of
warehouses all along US 99W where the highway ran parallel
to the railroads. That's how they looked to me, anyway, but
to someone older, or to someone who had more of an aware-
ness of how human nature can take its dark and twisted turns,
even in a small town, the abandoned factory might have
looked just like what it was—a place where boys with an un-
healthy curiosity could meet with dirty old men.

It wasn't as if the town kids didn't know any better. In
the past few years, when we would go to the creek in the
springtime when the weather warmed up, we would see sul-
len, grimy men living under the bridge. We knew to stay away

from them. I never hopped any trains, but it was common knowledge that if a kid crawled into a boxcar and saw some hobo like that, he'd better get back out. The phrase at the time was that the tramp would make you be the girl.

So even if teen-age kids knew better, some of them went into the old milk factory anyway. Maybe it was for the thrill of doing something wrong and secret, or for the pocket money, or both. I didn't know of anyone in my grade who did it, but these two kids a couple of years behind me, Bonner and Preston, had talked about it, and so had a couple of others about their age and about their level—that is, the kind that got into trouble and ended up dropping out of school.

As for me, I knew just the name, Old Man Earle. The only time I saw him in person was when the woman in the grocery store called him Mr. Earle as she gave him his change. It ran a feeling of dread through me, and I kept my eyes away from him as he walked out the door. Still, I got a look at him. He had large brown eyes and a clean-shaven face with a sagging mouth. He reminded me of an actor I had seen in several westerns. He wasn't one of the better-known ones, as he usually played a secondary character, and I didn't remember his name. But I never liked his looks, not any more than I liked this man in the grocery story.

Old Man Earle, the old pervert, the old queer—whatever people wanted to call him. And he wasn't all that old—maybe in his fifties. Now he was dead. As near as I could figure it, they might have been hauling his body out of those musty old buildings two or three blocks away at about the same time I was having a lark with the forty-one nickels.

* * * * *

In the cool of the evening, after a dinner of canned macaroni and canned plums, I walked back into town. My current funds were at two dollars and one cent, but the bowling alley was a place where a person could hang out and not spend money. Lots of guys came and went in the course of an evening, and it was a good place to find out what anyone else was up to. For my own purposes, I was interested in finding out if there was any work around, and I had to admit to myself that I was also interested in knowing if Bonner and Preston were still in the can. I didn't think they would have killed the old man, but there are lots of things you don't know about your friends, especially if they're just casual pals to begin with.

Chapter Two

Two middle-aged couples, all in glasses and matching orange T-shirts, were bowling in one of the middle lanes. They were the only bowlers, but the corner where the younger people hung out had a small crowd. A guy named Morgan was playing one of the pinball machines, and two farm kids with flat-tops were watching him. Sitting at a table a few feet away, smoking a cigarette and drinking a bottle of Coke, was a guy I didn't recognize right away. He wore a thin, dark beard that didn't look like it was going to fill in very well. Perched on his nose was a pair of wire-rim glasses, the kind that had just become popular a few months earlier, during my second semester of college. When school got out and I went to Berkeley and be-bopped along Telegraph, I saw the style everywhere—round, rectangular, clear, yellow, or purple. So at first I took this guy to be from out of town, until I got a second look.

"Oh, it's you," I said. "Hello, Eugene."

"Hi." He gave me a matter-of-fact look, then seemed to recognize me. "Sit down, Larry. What've you been doin'?"

"Not much. School got out about three weeks ago, so I hitch-hiked down to Big Sur with another guy. He had a job at one of the lodges, but I didn't like it, so I came back. Meanwhile I met a girl from Walnut Creek, went over to Berkeley and saw all that with her."

"Did you go to the Haight?"

"No, I didn't."

"That's where it's happenin'."

"I guess so." After a pause I said, "What about you? What have you been up to?"

"I've been livin' in Sac."

"Workin'?"

He gave me a close look through the wire-rimmed ovals, as if he had decided I was on his intellectual level. "I've been writin' songs."

"Really? What kind?"

His eyes narrowed. "About life. You know. How plastic everyone is."

"Oh, yeah." I bobbed my head, like you were supposed to do when people said things like that. "So you came back home?"

He flared his nostrils as he took a drag on his cigarette. "For a while."

"Are you gonna write some songs about this place?"

"I could." His eyes tightened and his brows went up. "Unmask the hypocrisy of the upper crust."

It sounded like a phrase he had picked up somewhere, like the hat and glasses. "Hell, yeah," I said. "Might as well."

He pressed his lips together, then took a drink of Coke. "So how was college? Was this your first year?"

"Yeah. It was all right."

"Lotta girls?"

"Oh, for sure. But not like some guys would let on. It's easy to talk to them, but it's hard to get very far beyond that.

You get to know one for a little while, and then you find out she's got a boyfriend back home."

"They just say that."

"I don't know. I checked on a couple of 'em, asked their friends, and they said it was true."

"You hear a lot. Don't believe half of it."

"Sure. And not just girls. This one guy in the boarding house, to hear him tell it, all he did was win fights and lay girls. But I never saw any of it."

"I know guys like that. Couldn't get a piece of ass if they paid for it."

"I guess there's some of that in Sac."

"Whores? Oh, yeah. Right on the street."

I shook my head. "I don't know much about that. I've seen 'em, just drivin' by."

Eugene lifted his head with a kind of man-of-the-world air about him. "It takes all kinds."

At this point I saw that he had a shiny, narrow cane leaning against the inside of his right leg. I remembered he had a catch in one leg that kept him out of the draft, but I didn't remember him having to use a cane, so I wondered if it was part of his songwriter get-up.

After a moment he spoke again. "I guess someone killed Old Man Earle."

"That's what I heard."

He scratched his sparse beard. "Can't say it bothers me."

I shrugged. "I didn't know him." In the half-minute of silence that followed, I had a hazy memory that Eugene might have been one of the boys I had heard of in that connection.

He was a year ahead of me in school, so if he had had anything to do with the old man, it would have been a few years before the ones I had heard talk about it.

Eugene spoke again. "I guess they hauled in those two punks Bonner and Preston to ask them about it."

"Yeah, but I can't imagine them doin' it."

"Me neither. They'd need more *huevos* than they've got between 'em."

I thought he sounded kind of bitter, but I figured he was just putting them down because he was a few years older, a man of the world in his own eyes, and they were just small-town punks who hadn't gone anywhere or done anything yet.

Morgan was racking up games on the pinball machine, and the farm boys were cheering him on. Bowling pins crashed in the background. Eugene and I didn't say anything for a couple of minutes as he crushed his cigarette and drank the last of his Coke. I thought he was getting ready to go, and then Jesse Bonner and Darnell Preston came in past the counter and stools.

In light of the conversation I had just had with Eugene, these two kids did look a little silly, like rat-fink hoodlums in a beach-party movie. They had their shirts untucked and their collars up, and they walked leaning forward with their arms straight down, each of them with a cigarette in his right hand. Jesse was the shorter of the two, a sandy-haired kid with a soft face and a build to go along with it. Darnell was taller, darker, and thinner, so he looked a little more solid, except that he had a fuzzy black mustache trying to make an impression on his upper lip. Both of them looked like what they were, just kids, and I think they got some of that quality from having older brothers. Jesse's brother was about five years older, cool and slick, with a red Malibu and a floor shift, and a blonde girl who sat almost in his lap. Darnell's brother was about three years older, not so cool, but already married to a girl who was a year older than he was. I always thought he was a slow, humorless sort, but in Darnell's stories he was a legendary stud who banged this older girl all night every night they went on a date. And knocked her up, of course.

So here were these two sixteen-year-old kids strolling into the bowling alley, no doubt aware that everyone in town knew they had been taken in for questioning. I wondered if they thought it made them seem notorious or dangerous, or at least important, because they walked up to the table where Eugene and I sat, and they looked us over as if we were a couple of loafers sitting on a bench and shelling peanuts.

Darnell looked at Eugene and said, "I thought that was you. I didn't know you were back in town. I heard you were dead."

Eugene took out a pack of Lucky Strikes, the short unfiltered kind, and tipped it so that a cigarette slipped into his palm. Still with the same hand he took the cig between two fingers and stuck it in his thin mouth. After he lit it he shook the match and said, "I'm not dead till you read my obituary."

Darnell turned to his partner. "But it's true we heard it, didn't we, Boner?" He always called his pal "Boner" with that juvenile sense of humor that never seemed to die.

"Yeah, we did," said Jesse, "but I don't remember where."

13

Eugene wrinkled his nose. "It doesn't matter. But you can see it's a bunch of shit, whoever says it." He took a long, authoritative puff on his cigarette.

Jesse turned to me. "Hi, Larry. How long have you been back in town?"

"A few days."

He smiled. "Saw you earlier, but didn't get a chance to ask."

"No hurry." I glanced at Darnell and then back at Jesse. "At least they let you guys out on the street again."

Darnell spoke up. "Shit, we didn't do anything. They just pick on us 'cause it's the thing to do." He raised his cigarette and puffed on it. "They just wanta make a big deal out of it, but they got their head in their ass."

"I'll tell you," said Eugene. "If this was down in Sac, it wouldn't be a big deal. Things like that happen every day. But still, if you were down there, you wouldn't get out of the can so easy."

"Well," Darnell answered, "this isn't Sacramento, and we're not in the can. So whoop-dee-shit." He raised his cigarette and tipped his head back to take a big puff.

Eugene scowled. "You punks think you're smart, and it's all a big joke, but don't be surprised if they haul your ass back in."

Darnell stiffened. "Don't call us punks."

"I just did. If the shoe fits—"

"Ah, calm down, both of you," I said. "You don't need to start anything in here."

Eugene crushed his half-smoked cigarette. "I was about to leave anyway." With a little flourish of the cane he pushed himself up out of his chair. Then he hefted the cane in a light toss, grabbed it as if he was choking it by the neck, and sauntered out of the bowling alley with the cane raised at his side like a baton.

Jesse turned from watching him walk away. "That must be what happens when you go away to the city."

Darnell made a "Puh" sound and said, "The city. That's San Francisco or L.A. All he did was go to Sacramento, and come back lookin' like a pimp."

"How do you know what a pimp looks like?" I asked. "Are there any of them in *King Creole*?"

"What's that?"

"It's a hoodlum movie. I thought you guys watched it, and that was where you learned your moves."

"Aw, go on. You're as bad as what's-his-name, Ass-Eyes."

I looked in the direction where Eugene had gone. "He's all right," I said. "He just doesn't like very many people."

"I'm sure it's mutual," Darnell said. "I think he's a shit-face."

I thought someone should teach these kids to swear, but I wasn't the guy for the job. "So what else are you guys up to," I asked, "besides gettin' hauled in by the cops?"

Jesse answered. "Not much."

"I need to find some work," I said. "You know of any?"

"Nah. About the only thing goin' on right now is apricots." He looked down at the floor. "That's a slow way of makin' anything."

"It's all right," I said. "And you don't get your ass in the clink for it."

Jesse shook his head. "I don't like it."

His partner chipped in. "Ah, you break out in a cold sweat just thinkin' about work."

"I don't see you runnin' down to the labor office."

"Look," I said. "You guys need to make some money, right? Well, I do, too. We can go out and pick apricots together. If I can ride with you, I'll help pay for the gas."

"I thought you had a car," said Jesse. "Like a Buick or an Oldsmobile."

"I did. It was a Pontiac. But the transmission went out of it, and I was broke, so I had to sell it cheap. I've gotten okay at hitch-hiking, but that's not much good around here."

"It's a long walk out to any of the orchards."

"You're tellin' me," I said. "It's far enough just out to Shady Grove."

Darnell frowned. "You walk all the way from there? Are you stayin' in one of the cabins?"

"In a trailer."

"That's where all the hay haulers stay."

"Oh, yeah," said Jesse. "They sit in the store there, or whatever it is, like a bar, and drink beer and roll dice."

I'd seen them, guys with big muscular arms and their shirt sleeves cut away, slamming leather dice cups on the counter.

"Ship, captain, and crew," Darnell said, getting back into the conversation. "My brother said that's what they play there."

"Liar's dice," Jesse countered.

"Anyway," I said, "what do you guys think? Do you want to go to work tomorrow?"

They looked at each other and shrugged.

"You guys are goin' to be a long time makin' your first million."

Jesse looked at me with his pale blue eyes. "And you're gonna show us how, pickin' cots?"

"I'll be your moral support. We might not get rich, but if I go out there, it's to work. I'll make somethin', and if you guys don't sit on your ass all day, you will, too."

"Well, shit fire and save matches," Darnell said. "Why aren't we out there right now?"

"Morning's soon enough," I answered. "If you guys can get up before noon."

"We're on restriction," said Jesse. "We've got to be in by ten."

"That's fine. Why don't you pick me up at seven, then? I'm in the smallest trailer, a grey one with no car in front of it."

They went over to rail at Morgan a little bit, and then they left. They didn't offer me a ride, so I just sat there, thinking I'd leave in a couple of minutes and walk home.

As I was sitting there daydreaming, someone walked up on my left side. I looked around and saw Dennis Wilkinson, which didn't surprise me. He had been sitting at the far end of the counter, near the lanes, when I first came in, but I didn't pay much attention. Now I got a good look at him.

He was scrubbed as always, tall and clean-cut in a pair of slacks and a white shirt. I figured he'd gotten off work at the One-Stop Market, where he'd worked all the way through high school. He was a year ahead of me in school—the same year as Eugene, as far as that went—so he had just finished his second year of college. His girlfriend was a year behind me, so she would have just graduated from high school. She was part of the in-crowd, a blonde bouffant cheerleader and an insurance agent's daughter. Dennis wasn't as much in the in-crowd as far as I remembered, but he had a little money and a nice shiny '64 Chevy hardtop, and he was working his way up.

"Hi, Larry," he said. "Mind if I sit down?"

"No, go ahead." I wondered what use he had for me, but I was in no hurry, and I wasn't too good to talk to someone just because he wore too much Brut.

"How was your first year of college?"

"It was okay."

"Get through all your classes?"

"Oh, yeah."

"That's good. A lot of guys, you know, they go off to school and then they don't stick with it. They goof off, go down the tubes."

I shook my head. "I got through all my classes just fine. One *C* and the rest *A*'s and *B*'s."

"That's good. And what is it you're majorin' in?"

"I'm sort of in between. I started out in psychology, but it wasn't what I thought it was going to be, so I'm thinking of something else. Maybe history."

"That's good. I mean, that's a good area."

I shrugged. "I don't know. I guess I'll find out. How about you?"

"Oh, I'm majoring in business. Lots of opportunities there."

"I bet. You go to Sac State, right?"

"Oh, yeah. Good school."

No one said anything for about a minute, and then he spoke again. "Hey, I saw you talking to those two kids. I heard they were the ones that might have done in that homo."

"Nah, I don't think they're up to that sort of thing—not yet, anyway."

He fixed his brown eyes on me. "You can't tell. You hear of pachucos their age doing all sorts of things."

I waved my hand. "Oh, that's in the city. I know those two guys, and if they had done it, I think I could tell by the way they acted."

"Don't be surprised," he said. "You've studied a little psychology, at least, and you know people get shocked all the time by someone close to them, someone they think would never do a thing like that."

"I wish. I spent about five years thinkin' how cool it would be if the cops came and took my stepfather away for something hideous, but they never so much as wrote him up for expired registration. He even waved to 'em."

"Well, just mark my words. And by the way, was that Eugene Fillmore sitting here?"

"It sure was."

"I didn't know he was back in town, and in fact I thought I heard he was dead."

"Well, he's not, of course."

"I can see that now. What did he think of these hoods?"

"Oh, I don't think he believes they'd do it, either. He just made fun of 'em and called 'em punks."

"Like he has room to talk."

"Huh," I said. "I don't think he's ever been in trouble."

"Maybe they've never picked him up, but I'd bet he's got it in him. He's almost as low-class as they are."

I didn't like the tone he was taking, so I said, "Some people get a better start to begin with. You learn that, too. You hear it in one place or another, that if everyone started with the same amount, after a period of time there'd be some people pretty well off and other people broke. So not everyone's equal as far as hangin' on to things or acquirin' 'em. Along with that, you learn that some people just have more from the beginning, which means that others have less. That's one way of being low-class, but there are others."

"Oh, I know all that, and I didn't want to start an argument."

I could tell he realized he'd stepped on my feelings as well, and now he was being a nice guy again. "It's all right," I said. "None of it matters much. I know who I am, and you know who you are."

"That's right," he said, giving me an assuring nod he might have learned from his girlfriend's father if it didn't come to him naturally already. "The good thing about you, Larry, is that you're smart, and you think about things."

I thought he was going to try to sell me something right there, but he didn't. He stayed around for a couple of more minutes, then looked at his watch and said he had to work in the morning.

So did I, I hoped, but I didn't say anything. I waited until he was gone, and then I walked home in the warm summer night, past the last streetlight where three-inch June beetles smashed into the glass lens and fell to the pavement. There they lay on their backs, waving their legs at the stars and waiting to die.

Chapter Three

The apricot orchard was starting to warm up by the time we got our referral, found the orchard, and got set out on our rows. The picking buckets were the regular old kidney-shaped type that were called belly buckets, from the way they hung across a guy's stomach. The ladders were old ten-footers, painted white with a red stripe across each side rail at the five-foot mark. According to labor laws, no one under sixteen was supposed to go above five feet on the ladder. Bonner and Preston were both sixteen, so they each got a ladder as well as a bucket. I could tell they didn't like pulling the harness over their head and getting the straps straightened out. It meant work, and every time a guy stopped to lolly-gag, he had the bucket there to remind him.

I took one row, and they took the next one together. We agreed that if they got very far ahead, they could skip over to my row and pick a tree to help me catch up, but after we'd been at it about an hour I wondered if it might work the other way around.

We were picking by the box, forty cents for a fifty-pound lug box full of apricots. It took two buckets to fill a box, so if a guy was picking bottoms, he might fill his bucket all the way a few times. But if he was going up and down the ladder, he'd empty it rather than carry half a bucket or more up the rungs. That was how I did it, anyway, and I tried not to lose time whenever I did empty my bucket.

These other two, though, didn't have much of a knack for this kind of work, where you got paid strictly on the basis of how much you did. They would pick for a while, maybe a quarter of a bucket, and go empty it. Then they'd go back to the ladder, re-set it, and stand with one hand on each rail, looking up at the fruit. They'd pick what they got on that set of the ladder, then go empty the bucket again. They had barely picked a box each when they took a break, turning a couple of the field crates upside-down and plunking their asses down to smoke a cigarette and drink water.

I just raised my eyebrows and kept working. I'd seen worse. I remembered one kid in the prune orchards who had come from Arkansas to stay with his sister. Her husband was driving forklift, so he got the kid a job pickin' up prunes in the same orchard. I have to admit it would be pretty demoralizing to have to try to fill a three-by-three bin of prunes by yourself, but this kid was hopeless. He was sixteen, three years older than I was at the time, but he had pale, skinny arms like he'd always stayed inside watching t.v., and he wore cowboy boots and a straw hat. Partway through the first day he pooped out and sat against the trunk of a tree for the rest of the day. When his brother-in-law finished his shift on the forklift he helped the kid fill his bin, and that was it for prune-picking. For the next two days the kid rode around on the forklift, slouched on a wide running board, and after that I didn't see him again. I heard his brother-in-law got him a job driving a water truck, to keep down dust on the dirt roads around the orchard, but he wasn't any good at that, either. He filled the water tank at a slow trickle and went to sleep in the cab of the truck.

By comparison, then, my two pals weren't so bad, but they weren't going to make much more than cigarette money.

I decided I was going to take a break after my first ten boxes, so I worked non-stop as these other two would work a little, loaf a little, and so on. When I took a break, they joined me.

Jesse's mother had made egg sandwiches for the two of them to eat at mid-morning, but Darnell didn't want his, so Jesse gave it to me. It was good. It had salt and pepper and pieces of bacon in it. I shared coffee from my thermos, and we took turns using the plastic red cup. It was all kind of brotherly, as these other two had gotten dirty and sweaty in spite of their resistance to the work, and we were off doing honest labor in a hot, drowsy orchard where no one in the world was going to give us shit except the row boss.

As we sat there amidst the dirt clods and the faint sounds of other people working and talking farther into the orchard, these two kids started telling stories. Like most of the tales I had heard from them before, these were about things that had happened to other people. One story was about a kid their age, who hadn't been in town long and so I didn't know him. According to Jesse, the kid had run off with a woman who kept him in bed almost the whole time he was with her, which was about two weeks. When the kid was telling the story to a handful of his pals, one of the other kids asked if the woman was a hemophiliac. Jesse cracked up at this point and handed me the plastic thermos cup.

"He meant nymphomaniac."

"I get it," I said.

"And the kid it happened to, he said, 'I don't know, but she sure liked to fuck a lot.'"

Now Jesse and Darnell both busted up laughing. I imagined they had been through the routine a dozen times, and I wondered if either of them knew what a hemophiliac was.

From there they went to another story about some kids who took a girl out to an old airstrip in the country, where they took turns with her in the back seat. One kid, named Fred Tarin, whose family had a couple of dinosaur tow trucks and a wrecking yard, was taking too long on his turn. The back door at his feet was open, and the other kids would look in and tell him to hurry up. He would look over his shoulder and say, "Go away, I'm not done yet."

Darnell, who was telling the story, said, "Poor Fred. He was so dumb, I don't know if he even knew how to do it, and it was probably the only time he ever got to."

"Why do you say that?" I asked.

"Oh, he got killed in a car wreck a couple of months later."

"That's too bad."

Darnell shrugged. "Drivin' that '56 Mercury about a hundred miles an hour, I guess."

Jesse turned to me and said, "Don't you have any stories, Larry?"

"Well," I said, "I think most of the stories about gettin' pussy happen to other people. But I did hear a story that might be true. When I was out hitch-hikin', down there by Hollister and Gilroy, I met a couple of kids about my age. They said they'd gotten a ride with an old guy who had a wife who was a little younger and had big tits. She was drivin', and the two kids got in the back seat. They asked the old man if he had a road map, and he reached over and started rubbin' the woman's tits and said, 'What do you think about these road maps? Would you like to see 'em?' So the woman pulled onto a back road, and out come her big tits. The old man got out of the car to keep a lookout, and the woman got in the back seat and took on each of these kids. The old man watched, and he seemed to enjoy the whole thing. When it was done, they took the kids back out to the highway and left 'em off."

"Sumbitch," said Darnell. "I guess we should hitch-hike."

"I've thumbed a couple of thousand miles," I said, "and nothing like that has ever come close to happening to me. Like I said, these things happen to other people, or at least they say they do. I met a couple of other kids, down by Carmel, one of 'em had a Levi jacket just like mine. They told me how they'd gotten picked up by a priest or something—maybe a friar, because he took them to a place where a couple of these religious guys were living. Kind of like a convent. They told the kids they could spend the night there, and then they gave 'em some wine and got 'em kind of woozy. They showed the kids where they could lay down, and when they did, these friars or whatever started rubbin' their legs and so on. It scared the hell out of 'em, and they grabbed their stuff and hit the road." I looked at Jesse. "So maybe you guys are better off not hitch-hikin'."

26

He smiled. "I'd take my chances with the big tits."

I laughed. "That reminds me of something I heard last year when I was pickin' peaches over on the other side of the river. You know, we got paid by the bucket there. We dumped the fruit into bins, with four bins to a wagon. Each wagon had a sorter, to pull out the undersized and bad peaches, and a checker, to keep tally of how many buckets you picked. Anyway, the checker was an older Mexican woman who talked in a shrill voice. She'd holler at the Mexican guys in Spanish, then rattle on in English at the sorter girl, who was the tractor driver's girlfriend. And this old lady didn't care about her language. She'd say, 'An' I tole that sunnavabitch, you git outta my way you sunnavabitch or you be sorry goddammit.' One time I was steppin' up onto the trailer to empty my bucket, and she was talkin' about some woman in town that the Mexicans all knew. She says to the sorter girl, 'They all call her Big Tits.'"

I did the voice up nice and shrill, and I got Jesse and Darnell to laughing pretty good. I said it again the same way, and they laughed again.

When everything settled down and no one started a new story, I said, "So who do you think killed Old Man Earle?"

Jesse leaned forward on his crate and spit out a drool onto the clods. "No tellin'. No one liked him, but I don't know of anyone who hated him enough to do that."

Darnell said, "I wouldn't be surprised if it was your friend with the goofy glasses."

"Eugene? I can't picture it."

"It happened just about the time he came back to town."

"Well, so did I, but that doesn't mean I did it."

"No one said you did."

"Why do people say he might have done it, then?"

"Who else said it?"

"Oh, well, Dennis Wilkinson sort of hinted at it. But I have to say, he mentioned you guys first."

"Good old Pennis," said Darnell. "My brother said that when they were in the eighth grade, Pennis said he wanted to be an undertaker because they made so much money. He wouldn't play football because he didn't want to get hurt, but get this. He didn't like the way they got dirty, either. So he played tennis, where they wear everything white."

"He's a prick," said Jesse. "Dennis the pennis, who plays tennis."

"Well," I said, "it still doesn't answer the question of who killed the old queer. I don't see what the motive would be."

Darnell piped up. "For Eugene? The same one they tried to hang on us."

Jesse added, in an apparent imitation of an investigator, "For liberties he took."

"What's it to you?" Darnell asked as he looked at me.

"Nothin', really. Just somethin' to wonder about."

We worked through the rest of the morning, and along about noon I started to hear the other pickers calling to one another and then talking as they walked out to their cars at the edge of the orchard. Some of the kids from town were working out there, as we could tell from the cars as well as from their voices, and I got the feeling that Jesse and Darnell were in no hurry to go out and eat lunch in their company. As I

28

emptied my bucket into the box and leveled off the fruit, I looked around and saw my two companions watching me.

"How many's that?" asked Jesse.

"Eighteen."

"What are you goin' to do with all your money?"

"Oh, I don't know. I'm thinkin' of goin' into business for myself, set up my own office, get me a girl Friday—"

Darnell cut in. "You ought to get one that'll do it every day."

"You act like a moron," I said. "Haven't you ever read a book, or the Help Wanted ads? A girl Friday's an office girl, one that answers the phone, types letters, runs errands—a little of everything."

"What kind of an office?" asked Jesse. "Detective?"

"You've been watchin' too much *Dragnet*. She works in any kind of office. The main thing is, she's reliable."

"But what kind of office are you gonna set up?"

"I don't know. Depends on how much of a fortune I make here. Shall we go to the car and eat?"

Darnell spoke. "It'll be too hot in the car. Why don't we eat here in the shade?"

"There's shade there."

"I'd rather eat here."

"Fine with me," I said. "Who wants to go get the lunch?"

They looked at each other, and then Jesse said, "Why don't you go get it?"

"What the hell?" I asked. "Are you afraid I'm goin' to steal some of your apricots and put 'em in my box? You guys are like the little turtle in the joke."

"What joke is that?"

"Oh, it's from the fifth-grade joke books. These three turtles are in the drug store, eatin' ice cream sundaes, and it starts to rain. Two of the turtles tell the third one, who's the littlest, to go home and get their umbrellas. He says, no, he doesn't want to go, because the other two will eat his ice cream. They say, 'No, we won't. Just go get the umbrellas.' So he walks away, and they go back to eating their ice cream. After quite a while, one of 'em says to the other, 'I wonder what's takin' that little guy so long. Let's go ahead and eat his ice cream after all, before it melts.' About that time the little turtle pops out from the end of the counter, where he's been hidin' all this time, and he says, 'I knew you were plannin' all along to eat my ice cream. Just for that, I'm not goin' to get the umbrellas after all.'"

"That's hilarious," said Darnell. "But since you rode with us, it seems fair that you go get the lunches." He held out the keys. "Come on, be a good sport. There's some of those guys we'd rather not have to talk to."

I wondered if it was because the other guys would razz them about Old Man Earle or because Bonner and Preston owed one or more of them some money. I figured it didn't matter. "All right," I said, taking the keys. I set off toward the end of the row, following the tracks that had been worn into the disked-up clods when the tractor and trailer had come through to scatter the empty boxes. *And they want to be tough guys*, I thought.

Chapter Four

Rather than march right in the front door of the bowling alley, I decided to go around the block and come in by the parking lot, to see if there were any cars I recognized. The sun had gone down, but night had not closed in yet, so I walked in the dusk of one of the longest days in summer. I passed the olive plant, where I smelled the sour odor and saw the huge wooden vats with iron rings holding the staves together. I didn't see any rats, but I knew they were in there, under the platforms.

As I came around the corner of one of the five small grocery stores in town, I saw the east wall of the bowling alley rising against the grey sky. I had noticed in the daylight, a couple of days earlier, that the building had been painted in the last few months. It was the color of the inside of a cantaloupe—a dull, pinkish orange. This evening, as I walked across the empty parking lot, I saw that the wall was spotted with a thousand long-horned June beetles, which I imagined settled onto the stucco surface in the shadows of late afternoon. When night thickened, they would go smashing into street lamps, moving cars, and the plate-glass windows of any businesses with lights on. I had heard there were millions of them on top of some of the buildings on Main Street, and people told stories of the bugs being so thick on paved roads that they caused cars to slide off and crash. By comparison, I was seeing just a few, but it was a creepy-looking horde anyway.

Inside, a grey-haired woman in an apron was sitting at the counter on my right, adding up sales tickets by hand. Straight ahead, all the lanes were quiet, with the pins set up and waiting. On my left sat the business office, dark now except for the window, where a powder-blue bowling ball with swirls of silvery white sat on a little stand and rotated in the glow of a tiny spotlight. Past the office and back to the left, the pinball machine area was empty except for one person sitting at a table and smoking a cigarette. I recognized his black felt hat and wire-rimmed glasses.

He lifted his head as a way of saying hi, and when I got closer he said, "Go ahead and sit down."

As I took a chair, I noticed his cane in the same place as before. "Write any songs today?"

"Not much."

"Make it with any girls?"

"None to tell you about. How about you?"

I hit him with a line I had heard not long before. "I eat more chick-en any man ever seen."

He pressed his lips together as if he had to be patient.

"Don't you like the Doors?" I asked. "Or have you heard them?"

"I've heard 'em."

"Well, that's from their album."

"It's got a lot on it. I don't remember that one." He took a drag on his Lucky Strike. "Anyway, besides eatin' chicken, what did you do today?"

"I went and picked apricots. With your friends Bonner and Preston."

"I didn't know they worked."

"It's not always evident, even when they're on the next row, but we got through the day."

"Why do you even hang around with them?"

"For one thing, they've got a car and I don't. I need to get back and forth."

He gave a little shrug. "Take what you can get."

"Well, it's work, and I'm broke."

"Who isn't?"

It was my turn to shrug. "You could try it." I knew that all the way through high school he had lived with his grandfather, who got by on a pension, and I assumed he was staying with the old man now.

Eugene shook his head. "I'm not gonna do work like that. I don't want to ruin my hands. I'm gonna learn to play the guitar."

I looked at his hands, pale and slender. "Well," I said, "there's other jobs. This last year I washed dishes in a restaurant and brushed tables in a pool hall. Worst thing that happens is your fingers get a little green."

"Maybe you should brush tables in the afternoon and wash dishes at night."

I thought he was being kind of dry about people who worked, but I said, "That's one good thing about washing dishes. You get your hands clean. That, and you don't go hungry." I could see he didn't care about that topic, so I changed. "It got pretty hot in the orchard today. How was it here in town?"

"Too hot."

I imagined him going out on foot for a pack of cigarettes. His grandfather had an old '52 Plymouth, but Eugene just about never drove it. "Over a hundred?" I asked.

"Easy." He shifted his cane about an inch.

I thought I'd cheer things up. "Say, you know what you need? I saw one on *Dr. Jekyll and Mr. Hyde*. A walkin' stick with a round knob of a head, suitable for bashin' in the heads of aristocrats."

"You've got a lot of good ideas. Too bad you can't sell some of 'em."

"Oh, I just thought I'd humor you. You're the one with the ideas, about hypocrisy in a small town and all of that."

"I'm sick of this town. I've been back four days, and I'm sick of it already." His eyes had a glint to them, and his mouth turned down, bitter-like.

"Geez, if it's that bad—"

"Fuck these people," he said, with his voice seething.

I sat straight up in my chair. "Did someone—"

"Them and their small-time, jerk-water, toady-ass cops."

"What did they do?"

"Oh, nothing. They just come to my house, put me in their stinkin' cop car, and take me down to the station. They harass me for two hours and then let me walk home when it's as hot as an oven out there."

"They took you in for questioning, then? About old what's-his-name?"

Eugene gave me a hard stare. "I'll tell you because I know you don't have any part in the chickenshit stuff. But I think your little friends tried to put the finger on me, and maybe someone else did, too."

"Really?" It sounded as if he had worked up the idea of a conspiracy against him.

He took a huff and a puff on his cigarette. "I'll tell you this. I never let that old queer do anything to me. But I know who did, more than once, and they hate their self for it. And they know I know, and it makes 'em squirm."

"Did you tell that to the cops?"

"Shit. They think what they want to. I told them I didn't have the motive or the inclination. Truth of it is, I don't think I even have the nerve to kill someone like that."

"But you didn't tell 'em who might have a motive?"

"I can tell 'em any time. If they piss me off again, I just might."

As he crushed his cigarette, I thought of a couple of things he didn't say. One was that he had never done anything at all with the dirty old man. The other was that maybe he enjoyed having something over on someone else, and it wasn't just peevishness at the cops that let him sit on what he knew.

I didn't think I'd get anywhere by prying, so I took another approach. "You said last night you didn't think it was the punks, as you called them."

"I still don't."

"Then why do you think they tried to put the blame on you?"

"Oh, you can tell by the way the cops ask the questions. They gave me the impression that two different parties mentioned me."

"No, I mean, why do you think the punks would say it?"

He waved his hand. "Oh, to get the heat off of them, I guess. And they don't know all that much about it." He looked past me. "I'll tell you the rest later. It looks like they just came in."

I looked around, and sure enough it was Jesse and Darnell, dressed like the night before. They had washed away the dirt and the sweat from the apricot orchard, and they had slicked their hair with fresh pomade. They came cruising up to the table where I sat with the songwriter and potential snitch.

I turned my chair around to the side, away from the table, and waved at them.

"Hi, guys," said Jesse. "You the only ones here?"

Eugene gave a slow turn of the head. "What's it look like?"

"I didn't think you had anyone hidin' under the table."

Darnell chipped in. "There's extra benefits in that."

Eugene glared at him. "Maybe you know a lot about that."

Darnell seemed to catch some of his drift. "No more than you. Probably less, you havin' been to Sac and all."

"What's that supposed to mean?"

"Nothin'. You just seem to know more."

Eugene did his trick with shaking out a cigarette. "If I know anything, it's to keep my mouth shut about things I don't know enough about."

"What's that mean?"

"I think you know."

"Well, blow me down if I do."

Eugene put his cigarette back in the pack and stood up. "You're a smart-ass little punk, that's what. One of these days someone's gonna knock your teeth out."

"Not you."

"Don't count on it." Eugene had his cane by the neck and held it at waist level.

"Ah, you're just a little weinie."

Eugene lunged forward, swinging his thin cane in a way that wasn't going to do anyone any harm, but he bumped into the table and sent the ashtray rattling. I jumped up and stood aside.

All of a sudden the place seemed full of people. Two high-school kids had come in and stopped in their tracks, and the manager came pushing past them.

"Look here," he said. "If you've got trouble, take it outside."

"It's all right," said Eugene, calm now. "I was just leaving." He touched the brim of his hat and said, "I'll see you all later." Then with his head lifted and his cane upright by his hip, he marched out of the bowling alley.

The manager walked back to the counter, where I saw Dennis Wilkinson sitting in the same place as the night before. The manager stopped to talk to him.

Jesse's voice brought me back to the present company. "What was all that about?"

"Oh, he's just touchy," I said. "I think he had to talk to the cops, and he's pissed about it."

"Well, he doesn't need to take it out on us," said Darnell. "We didn't do anything to him. And it's not like he's the only one who's been questioned."

I shrugged. "It's none of my business anyway."

Darnell turned to his partner. "Gimme a cigarette, Boner."

Jesse fished into his pocket and brought out a pack of Marlboros, then a book of matches. After he handed them to Darnell, he turned to me. "I've got a question for you. Bein' a guy that knows how to read and write."

"I passed my driver's license test."

"This one might not be so hard." He took the cigarettes and matches back from his pal. "What does it mean if some-one puts on a postage stamp upside-down?"

"Not much, I don't think."

"Well, Prestone here says it means sealed with a kiss."

"I doubt it. If someone wants to seal with a kiss, he writes S.W.A.K. on the back where he seals it. They've been doin' that for years, probably since the war. I imagine they even kissed the envelope there. Real romantic."

Jesse looked at Darnell. "See?"

"Well," said the other, "I heard an upside-down stamp could mean the same thing."

"I don't know," I admitted, "but if it does, not everyone knows about it. I've licked stamps and put 'em on that way, just to be contrary, I guess, or non-conformist. One girl I wrote to, her parents took it as carelessness and disrespect. Went on about it. But I think they were already inclined to see me that way."

Jesse shook out a cigarette. "So there's no deeper meaning?"

"Not that I know of. Is it some clue you ran across, to solve the big crime?"

"No, it was just something Prestone came up with."

I looked at Darnell, who seemed used to being called by the name of a can of anti-freeze. "I could ask my girl Friday about it," I said.

Darnell frowned. "I thought you said she didn't work in a detective's office."

"I said she could work in any kind. And actually, she does show up in the murder mysteries, like in the cast of characters at the beginning of those Erle Stanley Gardner mysteries."

"I don't read 'em," he said, still kind of surly.

"Neither do I. Not anymore. At one time I read a bunch of 'em, though, and later I gave the collection to my girl-friend's mother."

"Do you any good?"

"Not enough." Then, wishing I hadn't gone along with his innuendo, I said, "It hasn't helped me solve the question of who killed the old pervert.

Darnell leaned forward and tipped his ashes in the ashtray. "I don't really care who did. All's I know is, it wasn't me. Or us."

Jesse shrugged. "I still don't know why they call her Friday."

"It's from *Robinson Crusoe*," I answered. "The guy who lived by himself on an island. He ended up getting a native to be his servant. Met him on a Friday, so that's where he got the name for him."

"That would be handy. We could get one to pick cots for us."

"They're hard to come by," I said. "He was a cannibal, and Crusoe had to kill another cannibal to save his life."

"That sounds like a lot of work."

"Not if you have a servant. You get him to bury the dead guy."

Chapter Five

We worked a couple of more days in the apricot orchard, without servants. When the original Friday came around, we got paid through noon of that day. I cashed my check at the One-Stop, where I bought some groceries. I gave Jesse and Darnell a dollar a day for riding with them, so we were all in good spirits by about 4:30 when they left me off at my trailer.

That evening I went to the bowling alley, where I dropped a couple of dollars playing the pinball machine. Bonner and Preston didn't show up, so I figured they had gotten someone to buy them some beer or Apple Jack and were off at one of the regular spots drinking in their car. I hadn't seen Eugene since the night of the little tiff, but that didn't surprise me. All in all, the bowling alley was pretty dead for a Friday night, so I walked home at about ten and went to sleep.

The next morning, I waited more than an hour for my ride, and the guys never showed. I started thinking of them as the punks. I imagined them sick as a couple of pups, reeking of sloe gin or some such poison. When I got fed up with waiting, I put my lunch away and walked into town.

I thought that if I could get Eugene to drive me out to the orchard, for a small price, I could pick up my lunch, get in a half day, and arrange with some of the other guys to ride with them. To hell with the punks. I couldn't depend on them, and if anything, I made less with them around.

I went to Eugene's grandfather's house, which was a low, single-story hovel with chipped asbestos shingles on the sides. The old man answered my knock on the door. He had yellowish, watery eyes and about four days' worth of white stubble on his chin. When I asked for Eugene, the old man squinted a couple of times and spoke in a creaky voice.

"I haven't seen him since day before yesterday. He went out in the early part of the evening. I don't think he went back to stay with his sister, because his things are still here."

"You don't have any idea where I could find him, then?"

The old man shook his head. "What is it you want to see him about?"

"I know of a little work he could pick up."

"Oh, he could use that."

"Well, I wish I knew where I could find him."

With his hand still on the doorknob, the grandfather said, "He did say something about a girl named Paula. Whoever she is, she might know something."

"Thanks," I said. "I'll see what I can find out."

I knew of a girl named Paula Reynolds, and she might be someone Eugene knew. She was in her early twenties, had been through some sort of a half-hearted marriage, and was back living with her mother. They lived in a white stucco house across the highway near the stockyards. As the sun climbed higher in the sky, I walked over there.

The front door was open, and I could hear the t.v. going as I knocked. Paula came to the doorway and looked at me through the screen. She was a drab-looking girl, or woman, with sleepy eyes and big knockers. She was wearing a sleeve-less white blouse and a pair of cut-off jeans, and I couldn't guess if she had combed her hair yet today. I knew she knew me, but she gave a half-frown as if to ask what I was doing there.

"Hi," I said. "I'm looking for Eugene Fillmore. I was wondering if you know where he is, or if you've seen him in the last couple of days."

She shook her head. "I don't know where he is. He stays with his grandfather, I think."

"I knew that, but he hasn't been around for a day or two. I wondered if he'd been by this way."

"I think I saw him earlier in the week, but not since then."

"Thanks," I said. "I just wanted to let him know about some work I know about."

"I'll tell him if I see him."

"Thanks." I wondered if she thought I was using Eugene as an excuse to knock on her door, but nothing more came of the conversation, and I walked away in the hot sun.

Back at my trailer, I ate lunch and tried to imagine how I could get out to the apricot orchard. Anyone who wasn't a deadbeat would be busy working, so I was probably going to have to wait until late afternoon or evening to try to run across someone.

The trailer was starting to heat up, so I turned on the swamp cooler and tried to relax. I told myself that maybe Jesse and Darnell would come by, but I didn't much believe it. I sat there and fidgeted, thinking about what I was going to have to do just to get by. In two days I was going to have

43

to pay rent again, and that was going to leave me with about fifteen dollars. I couldn't coast on that for very long. One thing I knew was how to get a job and make wages, but I didn't like having to depend on someone else. I sure didn't like waiting for these other two guys.

At about four I walked back into town, and in spite of the heat it did me some good to walk off my nervous energy. I didn't have a particular place to go, so I walked where I could find shade, first along a row of businesses on Main Street and then through a neighborhood lined with shade trees. I found myself going past Eugene's grandfather's house, and I saw the old man sitting in the shade of a sycamore tree.

I stopped and asked him if Eugene had come back, and he said no. I went on my way.

Next I wandered along and turned on the street where the laundromat sat casting its shadow on the sidewalk in front. There I paused and looked north, where the orange co-op and the olive plant sat back from the street. It looked like a hot, sunny trek, so I turned around, went another block south, and hung a right at the corner. Two blocks ahead, on the other side of the tracks, stood the abandoned milk factory with at least a hundred yards of shade.

I crossed the tracks in the hot sun and went on without hurrying until I reached the shelter of the building. I turned left, walked to the south end, and lingered a moment. Then I turned and walked in the same shade northward along the row of connected buildings. I took my time. I came to a set of cement steps that led to a solid metal door. I passed it and a hundred feet later came to another entrance, this one with a railing of grey pipe going up the middle of the steps.

Along the walls of these buildings, sometimes at eye level and sometimes higher up, metal-framed windows gave a blank stare. I could see through most of them, and the buildings looked empty inside, with overhead iron beams, freestanding iron framework, and iron braces attached to walls. I also saw stairs and catwalks with iron railings. Several of the windows had iron grates on them as well, so the whole place had a resemblance to a prison or a bleak castle.

For a moment it reminded me of a movie I had seen a couple of years earlier, called *Castle of Blood*. It was a black-and-white British movie, with a couple of young Englishmen characters. One of them makes a bet with the other that he can't spend the whole night in the castle, which is supposed to be haunted. So the other one takes the bet and goes into the castle at dusk. He spends the night wandering from one room to the other, where doors creak, curtains wave, and shutters bang. He even climbs into one of the beds for a while. Then, when the first light of morning starts to show, he gets a hell of a scare and runs through the castle, out the front door, and through the iron gate in front. There he stops still, heaving a sigh of relief, and the gate bangs shut in back of him. Not long after that, a couple of bobbies come along, and they see the guy still standing straight up in front of the gate, with an iron spike, part of the railing work, sticking out the front of his forehead. I have to admit that even though it was a dorky movie, it had some genuine scary parts and a good surprise at the end.

I put that out of my mind and moved on. Past the buildings with the windows, a cement loading dock ran for about a hundred feet along a structure that looked like a warehouse. A pair of sliding doors came together with a heavy chain and padlock. The building and the doors were covered with corrugated galvanized metal, all a dull grey.

Past the loading dock, the building dropped to ground level, and the ridge of the roof was six feet lower as well. The area on my left was no longer paved with concrete but was covered with gravel, with dry Bermuda grass growing through in patches. The building had no windows or doors, at least on the side where I stood.

This factory had been a place that processed canned milk, so at one time it would have had tanks for boiling the milk, machines for canning and sealing, rollways for labeling, a casing machine for packing cans in boxes, a conveyor belt for the full boxes, and a station where men stacked the boxes on pallets. One of the few times I had talked with my father when I was able to have an actual conversation, he told me about working in a peach cannery on the other side of the valley. He loaded pallets, and he said the guy who ran the caser sometimes put in just three or four cans, enough to give weight for the box to run down the conveyor. Then the guy stacking the full boxes, who was used to hefting forty or fifty pounds each time, would give his usual heave and nearly fall over backwards. It was a big surprise, and it could cause a guy to pull his back muscles or fall off balance. The guy filling the boxes, who was a smug son of a bitch according to my father, thought it was real funny.

Anyway, from the little I had heard here and there, I had an idea of what the iron beams and frames and catwalks were all about, and I imagined the building I had come to had been a kind of shed for forklifts and jitneys and maybe stacks of old pallets. I also figured it was the easiest to break into.

As this side of the building did not have any doors, I walked along about a foot away from the structure and ran my hand across each sheet of corrugated metal. Where the sheets met, they were nailed onto the studs with large-headed, rub-ber-shanked, galvanized nails. Some of the sheets rattled, but none of them lifted away from the frame.

Around the north end, where the strong winds of winter hit the hardest, the panels were looser. Then, about six feet from the far corner, I found a sheet that lifted away. I had to turn around and crouch, but I was able to crawl through.

It took me a minute or two, paused with my hands and knees on the gravel floor, until my eyes adjusted to the dark inside of the building. The only light came through the crack of a sliding door on the west side. Beyond that faint stream of light, a low heap lay on the floor.

I stood up and walked in that direction. I crossed the place where the light fell in an uneven streak on the gravel. Now my eyes were well adjusted, and I could identify the object on the floor. He was lying face down with his head turned away from me, but he was still wearing his wire-rimmed glasses. His hat and cane lay on the gravel beyond his sprawled left arm and pale, slender hand. I could imagine him saying, "This is a rotten deal," but he was beyond ever saying anything again.

Chapter Six

My visit to the police station wasn't as entertaining as the previous one, but at least they treated me decent. Once I told them what I had found, they sent a cop in a car to investigate while two others took me into an inner room to ask me a few questions and to get a statement.

The hardest part was explaining why I had gone into the old building. I didn't have a good explanation. I knew I had felt a compulsion, based on the various things I had heard in the past few days, plus the disappearance of Eugene and the non-appearance of Jesse and Darnell. The best explanation I could give was that I had a strong curiosity. When the cops asked me what I expected to find, I was able to say, in total honesty, that I didn't expect to find anything in particular. When they asked me if I expected to find anything at all, I said I didn't know.

During my interview, the other cop came back from the scene and confirmed the report of a body. Then the two who were questioning me asked if I had any idea of who might have a reason to do such a thing. A shadowy image of Darnell Preston came up in my mind, but I said no. I didn't think that either or both of the punks could do it, drunk or sober. Furthermore, Eugene had disappeared on Thursday, and the kids had picked apricots in their normal half-hearted way on Friday, with nothing more urgent, that I could see, than drawing a meager paycheck later that day.

As the cops plied me with questions, they made no mention of any connection between this crime and the other one, but it was as plain as the nose on President Johnson's face. His portrait presided over the interrogation room, just as Dwight D. Eisenhower's had hung in the principal's office when I was a boy. I didn't feel the authority or the wisdom now, though. I just felt my own unreasonable guilt at being with three different guys who had probably taken money from Old Man Earle, and I also felt guilty for being the one to find the body. After all, I didn't stumble across it in an open field or on the side of the highway. Even if I was following a subconscious hunch, I had trespassed and gone into a place where a body had been found not long before.

All the same, the cops didn't have a good reason to keep me. When they said I could go, they advised me not to leave town without telling them. They also told me it would be better for the case and probably better for me if I didn't tell anyone I was the one who found the body. I answered that it seemed like a good idea to me.

On my way out, I saw a cop, or a man in a uniform with no gun or nightstick, carrying in a tray that had three bowls of beans and a loaf of Wonder Bread. The clock on the wall read eight o'clock straight up, and I figured it must be the lunch or dinner hour on their shift. They would eat their beans and then call the coroner and the mortuary. For a moment it seemed heartless, but then as I thought about it I realized they had a few hours of unpleasant work ahead of them. It was not the first or the last time I was glad not to be a cop.

The sight of the food reminded me that I ought to eat something. I didn't feel like going home for the night, and I didn't want to walk out to the Shady Grove and back just to eat a Spam sandwich. I went to a place called the Coffee Cup Café, where I ordered the plate special, a hot roast beef sandwich that came open-faced with mashed potatoes on the side and gravy on top of all of it. After the main plate, I had a piece of strawberry pie. It felt good to be able to eat a decent meal and to pay for it with money I had made. I was still haunted by a sense of guilt for finding Eugene, and now I felt there was something unfair about my being able to go on enjoying life while his was all over.

But there was nothing I could do about his being dead. He wasn't going to pop up again and say it was a rumor. I knew that for sure. I had to get on with my own affairs, look out for my own ass as the cops suggested, and keep my eyes and ears open in case something came out. Meanwhile, maybe the cops would haul in the right person. Now that I thought of it, they might not be all that dumb. They had convinced me to keep my mouth shut, and they must have done the same with whoever found the old man's body.

* * * * *

The bowling alley had a little life to it when I walked in. Half a dozen of the lanes were busy, with people chattering, balls rolling, and pins crashing. Over in the corner, two guys were playing pinball, each one banging his machine and shaking it, racking up points with pings and whirrs and clicks. Morgan the old hand was standing by watching. When he saw me, he turned and came my way.

Morgan was a year or so older than Bonner and Preston and a year behind me in school. He had dark hair, combed up in a wave in front and slicked back on the sides. In spite of a rough complexion, thick eyebrows, and a heavy shadow where he shaved every day, he had an open, carefree expression. He got along all right with most people, but he was probably not going to get very far in life. He had been in and out of juvenile hall for truancy, petty theft, drinking, and leaving home without permission, and then he dropped out of school. He worked when he had to, usually as a fry cook or dishwasher.

This evening he had less of a smile than usual, so I asked him what was up.

"I guess Bonner and Preston got run in again."

"Really? What for?"

"They found, or that is, someone found Eugene Fillmore in the old milk factory. Dead as a mackerel."

"Really? And the cops think these kids did it?"

Morgan shrugged and raised his cigarette. "Don't know what they think, but they hauled their asses in."

"So Eugene's dead?"

"Yeah, he was missin' for a couple of days, and someone said they thought he left town because he killed the old queer."

"Well, that theory sure doesn't hold up. Why do they think Jesse and Darnell might have done in Eugene?"

"I guess they had some kind of a fight with him, in here, just before he turned up missing."

"Oh, it wasn't that much. I was here. As far as that goes, Eugene was the one who got pissed off. The other two went on their usual ways. I picked apricots with 'em for two days after that, and I didn't see anything out of the ordinary."

"The other theory is that they killed him so they could frame him for killing the old man, and he couldn't deny it."

"That doesn't make sense. Not to me, at least. As Jesse would say, it's a lot of work. Not to mention bad strategy. Be suspected for one crime, and then commit another one just like it."

"Well, that's what's goin' around, anyway."

One of the pinball machines went quiet, and after a couple of routine curses, the guy who had run out of games told Morgan it was his turn.

"I'm up, Larry," he said, and turned to claim his machine.

"O.K. Good luck."

"Thanks. But I think those other guys need it more than I do."

I went over and stood at the fringe to watch the pinball players. The guy who had just run out of games was watching, too, and in a few minutes a couple of other kids drifted in. Morgan had a good touch for the game, and people liked to watch him. He could rack up enough games to go for quite a while, and even if a bystander got impatient or envious, deep in his heart he liked to see a fella beat the machine. I know I did, even on a small scale. More than once I had seen Morgan step into a phone booth, check the coin return, and come out with a nickel or a dime. Even though I knew it didn't take any talent, I enjoyed seeing him have success. And with the pin-ball, it did take some talent, or at least ability.

A few more young guys drifted in, some of them the smoke-at-lunchtime and missing-front-bumper variety, and some of them the football and chrome-rims variety. But the same topic buzzed back and forth. Eugene Fillmore had been found dead, and Jesse Bonner and Darnell Preston had been hauled in for it. Mention of Old Man Earle floated through, along with re-hashes of the flimsy motives Jesse and Darnell were supposed to have had for the latest crime. They did it out of anger, they did it to frame him. They did it because Eugene was a queer. I had a hard time keeping my mouth shut, but I figured the best way to keep from saying the wrong thing was to say as little as possible.

By and by I noticed another person taking it all in. Dennis Wilkinson stood not too far from me, wearing a collarless surfer shirt and a spotless pair of tan corduroys.

"Hi, Larry," he said, moving over so he was within easy range. "What's up?"

"Not much. And you?"

"I just left off my fiancée and stopped in here. We had a date, and she had to be in early tonight."

"I see."

"Have you heard this new stuff that's goin' around?"

"Some of it," I said. "You never know how much to be-lieve."

"Well, it doesn't surprise me. I knew those two kids were no good. I told you so, in fact."

"So you think they did it?"

He shrugged. "It seems to fit."

I shook my head. "I still don't see it."

"Ah, you were here the other night, when he took a swipe at 'em."

"Bah. I just don't see where that was enough motive."

"That's just it. At first I thought Eugene might have done in the old homo, for things that went on between 'em, and I still wouldn't rule it out. But it seems now, that if you look for what the two things have in common, these two hoods just don't have any conscience, and they pull stuff like that for trivial reasons."

"Oh, that's preposterous."

"Maybe you know something I don't," he said. "Bein' friends with him and them both."

I resented the remark but let it go. "I can't say that I know anything, but I don't think they were that mad at him, I don't think they wanted to frame him or even had a reason to, and I don't think they killed him because he was queer."

"Well, they're your friends."

His smug tone got to me now, and I felt like punching him right there. But what little judgment I carried around with me helped out. For one thing, he was bigger than I was. For another, I didn't need to be starting trouble myself. I'd been to the cop station twice in the last week, and both times I left on good terms. There was no reason to spoil that, much less give anyone the impression that I knew anything more than the next guy in the bowling alley, and I felt as if I had already said too much.

"Forget it," I said. "As far as that goes, I was a little pissed at them anyway. They were supposed to pick me up for work, and they didn't. So I missed a day's wages."

"That's too bad. I didn't know that. Hell, you could have called me."

"I don't have a phone. I'm staying out at Shady Grove."

"Oh, I didn't know that either." He was being friendly and considerate now.

"Yeah. You know, my mom and my step-dad moved to Oroville so he could work on the dam."

"I guess I knew that but I forget it."

"Anyway, I'm on my own. I like it better anyway."

"Sure. You can do as you please."

"I'm used to it."

"Oh, yeah," he said, absent-like. Then he frowned. "Does that mean you walk into town and back?"

"Yeah."

"Well, hell, if you ever need a ride, let me know."

"I might. Like if I buy a fifty-pound bag of potatoes or something." I imagined him in his green apron.

"People do that."

"I know. I've seen 'em."

He moved on to talk to a couple of guys his age, one of them a jug-eared fella who had gone off to a junior college, flunked out, and gotten drafted. The guy's name was Walker. He had a high-and-tight, as they called the military buzz cut, and he was good at snapping his Zippo lighter. To my surprise, he offered a cigarette to Dennis and lit it for him.

It was well past ten by now, and I had had enough of the bowling alley for one night. Usually I could find someone to joke with or joke at, but it looked as if I was going to have to wait for some other time for that. I wandered off to the rest room, and when I was done there I went past the powder-blue bowling ball, silent in its endless rotation, and then stepped out into the night to go home.

It was dark as I walked along the old highway, and I kept well off to the side. Even though most of the L.A.-to-Portland traffic was taking the new freeway, some kind of a vehicle came up behind me every minute or two. Because the main part of town was on the same side of the highway as the Shady Grove cabin court, I walked on that side, which was the east side, whether I was going to town or going back. On this night, the headlights from the cars coming up on me made my shadow look large and grotesque as it grew, came toward me, and moved to my right each time. The weeds in the ditch and on the other side had grown up and dried out for the season, and I wondered what my shadow would look like to some cat or varmint crouched there. I fancied that it looked like the shadow of a low-flying hawk, but in reality I figured I was not striking much fear into the hearts of any skunks, opossums, or stray cats. After all, I was just a kid in tennis shoes, crunching along, as each car rushed by and faded away, its lights becoming dots in the distance as the chirping of the crickets filled the night again.

* * * * *

The next day being Sunday, I didn't know if the crew was working in the apricot orchard, and I didn't want to ask someone like Morgan or Dennis Wilkinson to drive me all the way out there, just to learn that it was a day off. So I frittered away the morning and the first part of the afternoon, thinking that if I didn't see Bonner and Preston by the evening, I would have to find some other way of getting to the orchard and picking up where I left off.

In the late afternoon I walked into town, and for lack of anything better to do I wandered up and down a few shady streets. As I did, I heard a car roll up behind me as someone called my name.

It was the two wayward teenagers, not looking any more like murder suspects than the last time I saw them. Darnell was driving, and Jesse was leaning on the window frame on the side near me. I stepped off the curb and walked toward the car.

"What are you guys doin'?" I asked.

Jesse flicked his ash out the window and said, "Just trollin'."

"For what? Carp?"

"Quail."

I thought they might go a long time before they had any luck there, but I figured he was saying what he thought he was supposed to. "I missed you guys yesterday," I said. "I hope they didn't give away our ladders and buckets." I looked through the window and across the seat at Darnell. "Are you guys plannin' to go out and give it another try tomorrow?"

"Might as well," he answered. "Nothin' better goin' on."

"And Lord knows, we could use the eggs," Jesse added.

I didn't recognize that line, but it sounded like it came from somewhere. "Do you want to pick me up at seven, then?"

"Sure," said Jesse. "Do you need a ride anywhere now?"

"No, thanks. I'm just killin' time. I'll let you guys go on about your depredation."

"What's that?"

"Look it up in your Funk 'n' Wagnalls."

"I don't have one," he said, in a kind of stonewall answer that made me think he didn't know what a Wagnalls was.

* * * * *

They showed up at seven in the morning, and we got out onto the highway and headed north. It felt and looked like a Monday morning. On the right side of the highway, the gates of the junk yard had swung in, and farther up on the left, Seligman's fruit stand was opening for the day. As we drove past, I saw Kathy Seligman, who was about a year younger than my two comrades, setting out gallon jars of green olives on the wooden shelves beneath the canopy.

I remembered a couple of years earlier, and before that, when she wasn't even in junior high, she used to stand out in front of the fruit stand and give the finger to people she knew as they drove by. One time I was with the Nelson brothers, and she stood right out on the edge of the highway with her finger raised for the whole world to see. "Fuck you, Nelsons," she hollered. They said she did it all the time.

As we drove by, I asked my pals in the front seat, "You guys ever get any of that?"

"Not on your life," said Jesse. "I wouldn't do it with Prestone's dick. She's the meanest bitch around."

Darnell looked over his shoulder and said, "I heard she's knocked up. Strapped on one of your hay haulers."

"They grow up so fast," I said, in the tone I'd heard so many older people use, but I didn't see where either of the other two caught it. I hadn't gotten a good look at her just now, and I remembered her as a pudgy girl with no curves. The idea of her having any sex appeal mystified me. "By the way," I added, "Didn't Old Man Earle use to work in their truck garden?"

"Oh, yeah," Jesse answered. "But her folks didn't let her go anywhere near there. They had some other cases work there, too, like Lanny Marr."

I remembered him, the half-wit who looked like Walter Brennan. When he walked along the sidewalk, he turned around every twenty paces or so to see if anyone was following him. I would have thought that going out into the world as I did, and hitch-hiking, I would have met so many weirdos that Willow Fork would seem like Father Flanagan's Home for Boys. But now that I was back, it seemed that this little place had at least its share of strange ducks, and what impressed me as well was how Bonner and Preston took it all as normal.

Out at the orchard, we found where someone had picked the rest of our two rows. Our ladders and buckets were gone, too, of course. We walked through the orchard toward the sounds of work—fruit falling into a metal bucket, the third leg whacking the steps when a guy pulled the ladder back to re-set it. We found the row boss, a short guy named Gus who wore a canvas cap and had hair growing out of his ears.

He gave my two companions a blank gaze, and then, look-ing past all three of us, he said they were about ready to finish up the orchard. They didn't need any more help right now, but we could go to the yard and pick up what we had coming.

We did that, and half an hour later we were rolling back to town. I had a check for seven dollars and forty-two cents, and the other two guys had about five dollars each. They didn't seem affected one way or the other, and I could think back, not too long before, when I might have shrugged things off as well. If life got boring or seemed at a dead end, I might put a few things in my traveling bag, put a dollar or two in my pocket, and hitch-hike somewhere. Then after getting stuck for half a day in a place like Salinas, I would go back and tend to business. Right now, though, I had things to tend to and no way to do it. I needed to make some wages, pay my rent, and see if I could do something more than live hand to mouth be-tween now and the time I went back to school. It seemed that I needed to do something else as well, but I couldn't pinpoint it. It wasn't until the punks left me off at my trailer, and I realized that no one had said a word about Eugene, that I got a clearer idea. I felt some kind of obligation, a sense of unfin-ished business. I didn't know what I could do, being broke and on foot and not having any authority in anything. But Eugene was a friend of sorts, and I thought I owed it to him to stick by him, whatever that meant, until things got cleared up.

Chapter Seven

By lunchtime I was pretty restless from sitting around in the little trailer, and in spite of how much I had told myself I was going to do extra reading during the summer, it seemed absurd to be trying to read Kafka in a place like that. If I'd had something by Vonnegut, maybe the time would have passed in a less torturing way. Pynchon was another. You could read him without understanding him, and at least it was fun. But *The Penal Colony* was too far out of touch, or I was too far out of touch with it. I closed the book of Kafka stories without having gotten very far on the day, and I ate the lunch I had packed that morning. Then I walked into town.

After working three days with the punks and losing two, I thought I should try looking in the newspaper for some other kind of work. I took detours to avoid going near the milk factory or the police station, and I came into the downtown area where a bar called The Sportsman's sat on one of the main corners. The leather-covered door was swung inward, and I could hear casual conversation and the crack of balls on a pool table. It must be nice, I thought, to sit in a cool barroom on a Monday afternoon, and I wondered what the men looked like. Old guys in khakis, young guys in crew-neck T-shirts and blue denim Levi's.

I turned and went east for a block and then south for a block, until I found the newspaper office. I went in to buy a copy at the counter, and as I was paying for it a heavy-set guy at one of the old manual typewriters turned and waved at me. Then he went back to pecking at the typewriter.

I recognized him as Bernie Tompkins, an easy-going fellow a year ahead of me in school. I knew he was majoring in journalism, and I figured he was home for the summer. I went over to say hello to him. He was pecking away, not much more gallantly than Officer Arnold, when I spoke out.

"Hi, Bernie. What're you doin'?"

He turned and spoke over his shoulder. "Just an o-bit."

"Anyone I know?"

He stopped typing and rotated in the swivel chair. "Eugene Fillmore. You heard about him, didn't you?"

"Well, yeah. I just forgot for a moment that someone would be doing his obituary."

"It's easier if someone stands there and gives me all the details," he said, in a matter-of-fact way. "But I had to go get some information from his grandfather and then fill in with what I knew. We were in the same class, you know."

"You seem to be cheerful enough about it."

"From where I sit, it's just another piece to write. And if I don't have someone choking up and sobbing, I get through it all right. Off the job, though, it's too bad about him. And I feel sorry for his grandfather."

"So do I." I watched him take a swallow from a sixteen-ounce bottle of Pepsi, and then I said, "Any ideas on who's responsible?"

"Oh, that's not for me. I don't do the police beat or the crime blotter. But it's hard to imagine what someone would have against Eugene."

"Someone apparently did, though. And I think the cops are barkin' up the wrong tree."

"You don't think those two kids did it?"

"Nah. I know them, and I knew Eugene. There just wasn't that much bad feeling between 'em."

He folded his arms across his chest. "What's your theory, then?"

"I don't know. But I got the impression from Eugene that he thought he had something over on someone."

"Interesting." With his arms still folded, he rotated an eighth of a turn in the chair.

From the way he looked at me, or rather seemed to look through me, I got the feeling I had said too much. I made a hand motion as if to brush things away. "Well," I said, "I'd better let you get back to work."

"No trouble. If you get any more ideas, let me know."

"Even if you don't do the police beat."

"Hey, anyone would like to be the first to get onto a good story."

"I imagine." I raised my hand in good-bye, and I walked out of the newspaper office.

I sat on a bench in front of the soda-and-dairy fountain on the corner, and it didn't take me long to read the want-ads. The only two jobs except for baby-sitting and hair-dressing were for an electrician and a truck driver. That left me out. I knew a lot of people heard of jobs just through word of mouth, so I figured I was going to have to ask around. According to wisdom, Monday was supposed to be a good day to get a job, but it was pretty late in the day, and I didn't have a good start.

A fellow had to have his name out, plus a phone number if he had one. Maybe I could get someone to use for a message number—someone like Morgan, who wouldn't mind driving out to tell me and who might even take me to see about the job. That was it. I could get a message number, then ask around and leave my name.

At least I had a plan, but I was still restless. The whole business about Eugene was eating on me. I didn't like the way Dennis or Bernie talked about it, or the way Jesse and Darnell didn't. I had no idea of whether there would be a funeral, and if so, where. That kind of information usually appeared in the obituary, and the paper wouldn't be out till Wednesday.

The thought nearly stopped me in my tracks. For the first time, I remembered Eugene telling the punks they would know he was dead when they read his obituary. I doubted they would even read it, and furthermore, they already knew he was dead for sure if they were brought in for questioning. It was the type of situation that if it had happened to someone a little more distant, there would have been a joke in it, but the whole world seemed like a pretty humorless place for the moment.

I walked on, trying to think of anyone else in this town who might give a damn. I found myself walking in the direction of a white stucco house across the highway near the stockyards.

As before, Paula came to the screen door when I knocked. The t.v. was going, and I could smell cigarette smoke.

"Hi," she said. "I guess you heard about Eugene."

"Yeah, I did. Has anyone been to talk to you?"

"No, why?"

I shrugged. "I don't know. I just wonder if anyone's going to any trouble at all about it."

Just then the phone rang. "I need to get that," she said. "Do you want to come in out of the heat?"

"I guess."

The phone rang again. She pushed the door against the spring-loaded latch, and it popped open about an inch. "Come on in," she said as she headed for the phone.

I stepped inside, where the lights were off and a black-and-white t.v. was playing a quiz program. Three contestants were trying for a refrigerator, and the crowd was shouting, "Higher, higher."

Paula came back and pointed at the couch. "You can sit down if you want."

She was dressed as before, in a white sleeveless blouse and a tight pair of cut-offs. She had a full bosom and rounded hips, and she didn't seem to be guarding any of it with much suspicion.

I sat at one end of the couch, and she sat at the other. She lit a cigarette and offered me one. As I shook my head, I noticed that she smoked Marlboros.

"I didn't know him very well," she said. "He just came around, was all. Said he wanted to be a songwriter."

"That's what he told me, too."

"He said he wanted to get out of this town for good, but everyone says that." She blew a cloud of smoke out in front of her, then turned to look at me. "What do you do?"

"Oh, I'm looking for work right now. I came back for the summer."

"You went to college, didn't you?"

"I just finished my first year."

"I was never smart."

"Sometimes I think I am, and it doesn't do much good."

She gave a shrug. "There's no harm in it." Then she made as if she was scratching her thigh, and she moved the fringe of her cut-off about two inches toward her hip.

My heart started pounding, and I felt a swelling in my throat. I couldn't think of a thing to say.

"What do you learn in college?" she asked.

I felt dazed, and I heard myself say, "Oh, different things. Psychology, history, philosophy. Read books."

"What are you going to be, a lawyer?"

"Oh, I don't know. I haven't decided yet."

"Do you want some iced tea?"

"No, not now, thanks."

"You sound nervous."

I guess I was. I was shaking, and I could feel my voice quavering. But I said, "No, I'm fine."

The t.v. chattered on and seemed to fill the living room until she rubbed her thigh again. "What did you learn from those college girls?"

I pulled in a quick breath. "Nothin', really."

"Nothin'?"

I shook my head. "No. It wasn't a good year for that."

She moved her shoulders and sort of brandished her boobs. "That's too bad. Where are you going to learn the things you need to know?"

I swallowed hard. "I don't know. Wherever I can, I guess."

She pretended to frown. "You don't learn it all out of the book, you know."

"Oh, I know."

"Don't be so afraid."

"Afraid of what?"

"Of me. I'm not going to bite you."

"Well, I wouldn't want you to think I'm afraid."

She patted the space on the couch next to her, and I scooted over. I wanted to bury my face in her boobs, but I waited for her to say something.

"I bet your teachers in college aren't like this."

"Not at all."

"What kind of a teacher do you think I would be?"

My mouth was dry, but I was able to say, "Pretty good."

She turned her face directly toward me, and my lips met hers in a wet, smoky kiss. My right hand was on her waist, and my left hand was rubbing the points of both her breasts.

She got up, went to the door, and swung the little hook around and settled it in the eye. Then with the entry door still open, the t.v. playing, and the cigarette burning in the ashtray, she held out her hand to me. I rose from the couch and followed her into the bedroom.

It wasn't soft and perfume-y, but it was a woman's room, with a bed and a dresser and a chair, and nothing distasteful to make me wish I hadn't gone in there. In no time at all we were between the sheets, and she was pressing my face into her large, luscious breasts. Then I was on top of her, and in her, and moving with a rhythm I had never known before. I was lost in the swirl of it all, and when I was finished and was still lying on her with my face in her pink breasts, I wondered if this was what it was like for the two hitch-hikers who did it in the back seat with the woman whose husband looked on.

When I rolled onto my side, she said, "How was that?"

"That was terrific," I said.

"Have you ever done it before?"

"Just a couple of times, but it was nothing like that."

"A lot of those girls don't know anything yet."

Now that I was catching my breath and getting my thoughts back, I realized she must have been one of those women who liked to break in younger guys. I said, "That's why you're a good teacher."

She smiled and said, "You think I am?"

* * * * *

After we had done it a second time, we lay apart under the thin sheets. We were both perspiring from the exertion and the summer heat, and I uncovered one arm and one leg for some ventilation.

"Did you really come to ask about Eugene?" she asked.

"I guess so. I didn't have a real purpose in mind, but you seemed like a person I should talk to. I haven't been satisfied with the way people are treating this thing."

"You mean, not tryin' to find out who did it?"

"Well, that, and how they connect his death with the one that happened last week."

"You mean the old queer."

"Um, yeah. Old Man Earle."

"How do they connect that?"

"Well, one theory is that these two kids, Jesse Bonner and Darnell Preston, did in both of them for practically no reason."

"Bah," she said, "those kids aren't up to it."

"That's what I think, too, and I don't like anyone and everyone hangin' the blame on them, for lack of a better idea. And meanwhile, if someone else did do in Eugene, I don't like them goin' free. It's not right."

"No, it isn't."

"You know, they say the truth always comes out. I don't know if it does, but I do know there's a truth to this, an overall truth, and I wish people were doing more to get at it."

"Maybe they are."

"I don't know. There seems to be an attitude, and not just with the cops, that as long as they've got two suspects, that's good enough until a better suspect comes along."

"Huh." She shifted her body but did not move toward me. "You said one theory was that these kids did in both of 'em. What's the other theory?"

"I heard it side by side with the first one, as if they could both be right. In this one, Eugene killed the old man because of things in the past, and the kids killed him just out of anger, because of a little squabble they had in the bowling alley."

71

She cleared her throat. "Well, as for Eugene, I didn't know him very well, but he didn't seem like the type to kill someone. And how much of a reason would he have?"

"No more than the two punks. Supposedly the old man took some liberties with him as well as with them, but Eugene told me he never let the old creep do anything to him. I took that to mean contact, as opposed to watching while the old man exposed himself or whatever."

"If that's what he said, it was probably true."

"That's the way it seemed to me. And I don't think these kids did anything except watch, either, or maybe touch at one time. They said the old man would give 'em fifty cents, and this was, I don't know, three years ago."

"That was it," she said. "And he was doing it before the milk plant ever closed down. He'd give those kids fifty cents to watch him expose himself and play with himself, and he'd give 'em five dollars if they'd let him suck 'em off."

She didn't mince her words. If some guy in the bowling alley had said the same thing, I would have found it revolting. But with her, it was clear that she was talking about a different world than the one she and I were in.

"The hell," I said. "All I ever heard about was the fifty cents. I don't think Jesse and Darnell ever got out of that bracket."

"Well, the five-dollar stuff happened. I heard about it more than once."

"Eugene said there were guys who let the old man do more, but he didn't give details and he didn't say how much."

"Oh, yeah, there were others," she said. "But you'd never get 'em to admit it, especially now."

"I bet. It's like the old saying, dead men don't tell tales."

"Ah, that old queer wouldn't tell anyone anyway. It would be his ass."

"I suppose so." I didn't say any more, but I was thinking about something Eugene had said. I didn't know if he meant one person or more, but whoever had gone in for that stuff, he said they hated themselves for it and they knew he knew it. Maybe they hated him, too, for not having gone that far as well as for having something over on them.

"Don't be so quiet," she said. "Do you want a cigarette?"

"No, thanks."

"I'm gonna go get one." She rolled out of bed, went to the living room, and came back smoking a Marlboro. "I think you're going to have to get dressed," she said. "My mom gets home at a little after five." She sat on the edge of the bed, and with the cigarette in her mouth she put her bra on backwards so she could hook it in front of her.

"You ought to let me help you with something like that," I said. I was sitting on my side of the bed looking back at her.

"Guys are clumsy like that."

"Some of us are good learners. Don't you think?"

She smiled over her shoulder. "You're all right, honey. You came along just fine."

"I hope it's not all said and done in one lesson."

She pulled her bra up into place, put the straps over her shoulders, and pooked her boobs out. "It doesn't have to be."

73

"That's good." Even though her movement and her words sent a wave of excitement through me, I knew I was going to have to make hay while I could, because even this pleasure was going to have an expiration date. On the other hand, for once it wasn't something that just happened to someone else.

Chapter Eight

When I got back to my trailer, it was hot and stuffy inside, and the cooler was gone. I understood this development to mean that the rent was due, so I dug into my stash of money and went to get the cooler out of hock. I found it a little embarrassing, but the heavy-set guy who ran the place treated it like normal business. I lugged the unit back to my trailer and got it to churning the air. Another week, I thought, and if I didn't find some work, I might be looking at moving out on my rent.

* * * * *

Going to the bowling alley that evening was a good idea, insofar as I ran into Morgan. A couple of other guys were on the pinball machines, and he was just standing by, looking half-interested. He said he had gotten off work a little while ago at the Highway 99 Café, where he washed dishes. I believed him, because he had the smell of a restaurant kitchen about him. He was wearing a white t-shirt that sagged, and I could picture him working in the steam and over-spray of the big sink and the dishwashing machine, maybe with a stained white apron covering his pack of Winstons.

I asked him about using his home phone for messages, and he said he thought it would be all right. He would tell his mom. I went on to explain that I didn't want to use the Shady

Grove number because I didn't think the fat guy who ran the store and bar liked me very well. I said I could imagine the guy not wanting to venture out into the hot sun just to deliver a message, much less heave his ass off a stool if he was in the middle of a dice game. I didn't mention to Morgan that the fellow had found it in him to confiscate my cooler, nor did I mention that I wasn't sure how much longer I could afford to live there if I didn't find a job. One thing at a time, I thought.

Morgan nodded and said it shouldn't be any trouble. If something came up, he could let me know. He kept casting glances at the pinball machine, so I asked him if he wanted to go play.

"Nah," he said. "I already lost the change I had when I came in, and I'm gonna go home and get cleaned up."

"Maybe I'll see you later, then."

He didn't turn and leave, but rather shook out a cigarette and lit it. I was wondering if he was going to ask to borrow money, but he didn't say anything.

I spoke again. "Have you heard anything new about the murder case?"

He turned down the corners of his mouth as he shook his head. "No one says much to me about it, like at work. I guess it's because they know Jesse and Darnell are my friends."

"Yeah," I said. "People seem satisfied with the idea that those two guys did it."

Morgan raised his heavy eyebrows. "Who-all have you heard it from?"

"From Bernie Tompkins. He's workin' at the newspaper, you know. And then Dennis Wilkinson."

"Huh. Strange you should mention those two."

"Why's that?"

"I didn't think they were that good of friends, but they had lunch together today at the Highway."

That did seem like a mismatch, but it made a kind of sense. "I think Bernie wants to be Jimmy Olsen, cub reporter."

Morgan smiled. "And Dennis is Clark Kent?"

"Maybe something like that. How about you? What's your secret identity?"

"I don't know. What's yours?"

"Inspector Clouseau. Back on the Gambrelli case."

We both cracked up. *A Shot in the Dark* was one of the funniest things that ever came to this town, and it was always good for another laugh.

"Well, I'm gonna go," he said. "I'll tell my mom you want to use the number for job messages."

"Thanks. I appreciate it."

I hung around a little while longer, but there wasn't much going on. The two guys on the pinball machines ran out of games and left. It was about twenty to ten on a Monday night, and since I had accomplished the one thing I came back into town to do, I decided to go home. Tomorrow I could start over looking for a job.

I walked past the powder-blue bowling ball with swirls of silvery white, rotating in the glow of the little spotlight. Outside, the night was still and quiet. I had just crossed the railroad tracks and was halfway to the corner streetlight when a shiny white Chevrolet stopped on my left.

It was Dennis Wilkinson, so I opened the door on the passenger's side.

"Get in," he said. "I'll give you a ride."

The car was a hardtop and had white bucket seats. I slid in on the clean upholstery and closed the door. "Thanks," I said.

"Goin' home?"

"Yeah."

He stopped at the stop sign with the car angled to turn right. Then as he pulled out onto the highway, he said, "If you want a beer, there's some on the back floorboard."

"Oh, that's all right."

"Nah, get us each one."

I reached between the bucket seats to the floorboard in back of him and found my way into a paper bag. From there I found a six-pack that already had a couple missing. I took out one can and then another, not very cold to the touch. I handed one to him.

"They're pop-tops," he said. "Just pull the ring."

It being Monday, I imagined the beer was not left over from a date. If it had been riding around on the floorboard for a couple of days, it would be a lot warmer than it was. I assumed he had taken it out the back door of the One-Stop Market, where he worked, and had had it in the car for a few hours. When it came right down to it, though, I didn't care where it came from. I didn't have any money to spend on beer, and being under age, I was used to drinking beer that wasn't very cold. So I popped mine open and took a drink.

From the dash lights I could see it was an Olympia. "Thanks," I said. "This tastes all right."

"We'll drive out a little ways. No need to chug it."

He stepped on the gas, and we were going sixty as we went past the Shady Grove. The hay haulers' pickups and trucks were parked under the yard light, and of course my trailer was dark. Farther on, we passed Seligman's fruit stand, which was closed for the night. I expected to see Kathy out in front, one hand on her pregnant stomach and the other giving the finger in her vile way, but the parking area in front of the fruit stand was vacant.

Dennis turned right and drove out through the farm country, past alfalfa fields and almond orchards and orange groves. I rolled down my window, and I could smell the curing hay, the dust, the irrigated fields.

I took another drink of my beer. I didn't want to drink it too fast, but I didn't want him to think I didn't like it, just in case he had it in mind to offer me another one.

"So," he said, lowering his can of Oly, "have you been gettin' into Paula Reynolds?"

I was caught off guard a little, but I figured he must have seen me at about the time he got off work and I was going down her front steps and trying to make myself scarce. One thing I knew about girls like her was that even if they did it with half the guys in town, they didn't like being told on, so I said, "Not yet."

"Ah," he said, "you can get into her if you want. She's an easy make."

"Not that I noticed. But it's good to know."

"Just keep tryin'." He stepped on it and ran the needle up to eighty. "Do you have a cigarette?"

"No, I don't smoke."

"Oh, I guess that's right." He slowed down, turned left, and headed north. After a couple of miles he turned left again and headed back in the direction of the highway. "Go ahead and drink up," he said. "We've got two more to get rid of before we go back to town." He tipped his all the way up, then threw the empty out the window. With both hands on the wheel, he stepped on the gas again.

The Chevy took off smooth and fast. I watched the speedometer go to sixty, seventy, eighty, ninety, and a hundred. He held it there for about a mile and then let off. The car slowed down on its own, and when it was down to sixty again, he kept it there.

"If you're done, you can get us the other two."

I drained mine and threw the can out the open window. I didn't like to litter, but everyone knew you didn't keep the evidence.

With his second beer opened and in his lap, he drove on without talking. Then he said, "There's a lot of pussy in this town. Did you know that?"

"Well, I would guess so. It's just not all available."

"No, but there's a lot that is. And I can tell you how to get it. In fact, I know two girls that'll go out together. They won't go out one by one, but they'll go out with two guys. And they'll do it. Just give em a little beer, get 'em hot, and you've got it." He didn't say anything for a few seconds, and then he said, "You and I could do it. You know how to keep from blabbin'."

"Oh, yeah," I said, shifting in my seat. "But this is the last of the beer."

"We'll get some more. That's the least of our worries."

I took a drink of my second Oly and didn't say anything.

"We just need to kill these two before we get back to town."

I had heard great plans before, from one guy or another who knew where to get the beer, where to get the girls, and all of that. I figured I would drink this beer, and before we got back into town, I would ask him to leave me off at my place.

When we stopped at the highway, I took another good pull on my beer. He turned left and headed back to town.

"The main thing is," he said, "you've got to keep this under your hat."

"Oh, yeah. That's one thing I know how to do."

"I thought so, or I wouldn't have offered it."

He drove about two miles and then pulled off where there was a turn-out. It was a rest stop where a cement picnic table sat below a clump of oak trees. There was a dirt parking area on both sides of the table, and off to the right there was a border of oak brush. Dennis pulled the car over to the right side, near the brush, and stopped.

"Let's take a piss," he said. He tipped up his second beer just like the first one and threw the can out on the ground.

"Let me finish mine." I got out of the car and stood up with my eyes away from the headlights. As I was leaning my head back for a drink of beer, I thought I saw the car moving backwards. Then I heard the engine gun up, and the right headlight was coming straight at me.

I jumped, and the front part of the fender hit me on the hip and spun me into the oak brush. The car backed up, and I scrambled out of the glare of the headlights. I didn't know which way to move.

The car stood still. The driver's door opened and closed. I was waiting for Dennis to come around the front of the car, when all of a sudden he came out of the dark on my left side and tackled me.

By now I had an idea of what was up. He was the person Eugene had been smirking about, one of the guys who had been in the five-dollar bracket with Old Man Earle, and he had figured out I was getting too close to the truth.

When we hit the ground, he tried to get his hands on my throat. I grabbed his left wrist, shifted my weight, and rolled him off me. As I was coming up, he grabbed my hair with both hands. I drove at him, pulled one leg out from under him, and made him lose his hold. I landed to one side of him, and this time as I was getting up, he fetched me a hell of a wallop on the left side of my head. It almost knocked me down, but I staggered to my feet and kept my dukes up.

All this time, the headlights were shining for all the world to see, but not a single car came by. The two of us moved in and out of the glare of the right headlight, and a thin cloud of dust hung in the air.

He came at me, swinging, a dark shadowy shape in the dust and glare. I went under his fists, drove my shoulder into his mid-section, and tackled him. I got in two good punches until he threw me off. He got up before I did, and as I was halfway up and off balance, he grabbed me and pinned my left arm to my side. As my feet came off the ground I tried to swing around with my right fist, but he lifted me up and slammed me to the ground.

I hit the dirt hard, and I saw darkness with the little spots of light that people call stars. Then I realized I was lying in the beams of the headlights, and the car was backing up. It was like that kind of bad dream when you can't move, but it didn't last long. I rolled over, pushed up, jumped one way, then another, as the car came rushing at me, swerved, and crunched into the cement picnic table.

I couldn't see inside the car because of the glare of the right headlight, but when I heard the car door open, I lit out on a run. I got up onto the shoulder of the highway and headed for town. I was sore all over from the fight, and my hip ached where the fender had hit it, but I kept running. I thought I might be able to get a ride, but still no traffic came from either direction.

Looking back over my shoulder, I saw the car pull out of the picnic spot and onto the highway. Moving slow with one headlight put out, it looked full of vengeance. I knew from the low speed that Dennis was on the lookout for me, so I went down into the ditch and up the other side, then climbed the fence and headed out across an open pasture. I moved on a diagonal, and after I had gone about a half-mile, I stopped to look back. Dennis was stopped sideways in the middle of the highway, pointing his right headlight out into the pasture. He swept the beam in a small arc, then moved ahead a quarter of a mile and tried again.

I cut back to the highway and lay in the weeds until he got into position a third time. Then I went over the fence, crossed the highway, and took off for town that way.

I figured I was about three miles from town, and I knew it would be hard going as I went through orchards, across irrigated pastures, and over shaky fences. But that was the way I went, running on a cramped hip and an aching side, breathing hard, heaving deep, slowing to catch my breath, and running again. From time to time I could feel my head throbbing as well. The episode with Dennis seemed unreal, like another part of a bad dream, but the pain reminded me it was real.

For the last mile I ran along the railroad tracks, smelling the creosote of the ties and raking my feet on the large pieces of crushed rock. When I reached the edge of town, I cut over one block and jogged past the olive plant, the orange co-op, and then the laundromat. A block from the police station, a cop car stopped me.

Inside were Office Arnold and one of the men who had questioned me about Eugene and then let me go so they could eat their beans.

Officer Arnold, who had been driving, got out and came around to the passenger side where I stood. He looked me over with his five-cell flashlight and kept to one side so that the other cop could see me as well.

All the way into town, I had gone over how I was going to tell my story, so when they asked me what I was up to, the words came in a rush. As I talked, I was sure I looked a fright.

I was dirty and sweaty, with a scrape across my forehead. My hair was matted, grainy to the touch. My pants were torn, and the neck of my t-shirt had been pulled down to look like a V-neck.

I told the cops the whole story, from the time Dennis picked me up to the moment they stopped me. When Officer Arnold asked why Dennis would do something like that, I told them what I had heard from Eugene and from Paula Reynolds.

Arnold spoke again. "That's quite a story, kid." He ran his light over me. "I'd like to know what you're really running from."

"I told you. And if you don't believe me, you can look at the front left fender of his '64 Chevy hardtop."

"The fender he hit you with?"

"No. The one he ran into the picnic table. But if you want to see where he hit me, I can show you that, too."

Arnold looked up and down the empty street. "Go ahead."

I turned my back to the patrol car, undid my pants, and pulled the right side halfway to my knee. In the glare of the flashlight, I could see a reddish-purple bruise about the size of a small oval dinner plate.

Arnold held his light on it for a few seconds, then shined to the side before he clicked off the light.

I pulled up my Levi's and buttoned the front. "Well?" I asked.

"Get in. We'll go find this guy, take a look at his fender, and see what his story is."

Trouble in the Labor Camp

Chapter One

I followed the foreman's pickup into the labor camp and parked on the right side of the road behind him. I got out of my car and waited for him as he sat in the cab and lit his cigarette. As I had learned a few minutes earlier, his name was Len. He reminded me of someone I had seen before. It was one of those things I couldn't place, maybe something about his features or just the expression on his face. As he got out of the cab I saw it again, that look that said he was the foreman and I was just a laborer.

He waved his hand that held the cigarette. A row of four houses sat on the other side of the road. "That first house is empty," he said, "but you couldn't stay in it anyway because the floor's falling in. The second one has a Mexican family living in it, and the next one has a white family. The last house is empty, and I'm savin' it until another family comes along."

I nodded, and he turned to point at a quonset hut behind me. We had just driven past it and another one.

"You'll stay here," he said. "In the front half of the building. You'll share it with a man and his son. In the back half there's four young Mexican guys, brothers and cousins. In that other one there's a white family in front and a colored man with a white woman in the back half." He took a drag on his cigarette and said, "Follow me." He went up the steps and into the quonset where I was going to stay. He talked as I followed him. "This place has got running water, and each side has a kitchen area. Both sides use the same bathroom, here in the middle." He looked into one bedroom, where there were belongings all over the floor. He spoke with the cigarette in his lips. "This looks like Mack and his kid's room. Yours 'll be the other one."

I glanced into the room closest to the front door. It was empty. "Looks like this one."

"Yeah." He took the cigarette away from his mouth and gave me a steady look. "I shouldn't have to say this, but I will anyway. I don't put up with any trouble in my camp."

"I don't make trouble," I said. "I mind my own business."

"That's the best way to be." He raised his head. "Well, those others should be back pretty soon. You can go ahead and get settled."

He walked out, and a minute later I heard his pickup door slam and his engine fire up.

I went to the window of my room and looked out onto the road that ran through the middle of the camp. Len was parked in front of the third house, where a white woman stood on the porch smoking a cigarette. I couldn't hear voices, but I could tell they were talking.

I went back to the living room and took another look at the layout. I thought it was one of the better places I had stayed in for a while. It was clean, had solid floors and no broken windows, and didn't cost anything. Of course even at that point I knew, as they said about other things, that none of it was free.

When I heard Len's pickup rumble out of the camp, I went outside to my car. I paused for a minute and got a view of the quonsets. Mine was the second one on the right as a person drove into the camp. It looked as if the two of them had been put up where some even older shacks had stood at one time, as there were outhouses and piles of old pipe and lumber out back at the edge of the orchard. It all seemed normal enough, a place to stay while the work lasted.

I started unloading my stuff from the back seat of my car. As I came out of the quonset on my second trip, dust was hanging in the air above the road, and a car was pulling in on the other side of the second house. I heard car doors open and close, and I saw a dark-haired girl in work clothes walking around the back of the car and heading for the door of the house. It looked as if she had just taken off a scarf, as she had it trailing in her hand. It was a pale blue thing.

She glanced my way, and our eyes met for a second across the dust settling on the dirt road. Then she went into her house, and I carried a box of kitchen stuff into mine.

When I had all my belongings inside, I went to the bathroom and washed my hands and face. As I dried off and saw myself in the mirror, I recalled the dark-haired girl from across the road. As soon as I saw her I knew she was from the Mexican family Len had mentioned. Now I wondered how she saw me, whether she thought of me as a different kind of person because I was white, or whether she saw me as just another fruit tramp, white or otherwise, who followed the crops. I wondered how a guy like me could tell a girl like her that what he wanted was to work his way up out of this life, and I wondered whether she would think that was a good way to be or whether she would take it as an insult.

I went out to the living room and stood there listening. A car had just come in and parked between the two quonsets. I heard car doors, voices, then someone coming up the wooden steps. The door opened, and in came a man followed by a boy. They stopped short when they saw me.

"Hi," I said. "My name's Morgan. Len told me to move my stuff in here."

The man's eyes narrowed on me. "Yeah, he said we'd have to share." Then it seemed as if his face relaxed as he looked me over, and he said, "It's all right, though. We'll get along."

"Sure."

The man put out his hand. "I'm Mack," he said, "and this is my son Acie."

I shook his hand and nodded at both of them. Mack was a tall man with his head a bit large in proportion to the rest of him. He had close-set eyes. The centers were cloudy brown, and the whites were yellow and pink. He had a rugged complexion and uneven teeth. I was used to seeing people who had rough lives and looked beat to hell at forty-five or so, which he did.

Acie was about twelve years old. He was an overgrown boy, soft and weak, and he smelled of pee. He had straight blond hair, blue eyes, and a flushed white face that looked as if he had just finished crying or was getting ready to start.

Mack turned to Acie. "Go wash up, son."

"Yes, Daddy."

Mack took out a bag of Bull Durham and started rolling a cigarette. The drawl in his voice was noticeable as he bent his head. "It's a rough go. We been out here a while now. Come from Texas. My car gave out on me, and we ended up in this place. We ride back and forth with the old boy and his kids next door." He looked up and motioned with his head.

I didn't have anything to answer, so I said, "Uh-huh."

Mack finished rolling his cigarette and lit it. Acie came out of the bathroom.

"Ready, son?"

"Yes, Daddy."

Mack turned to me. "We're gonna go next door and eat with these other folks. They invited us."

"Sure," I said. "We'll see you later."

Acie gave me a whipped-puppy look as he walked past.

Except for his narrow eyes, I thought he was an unlikely son for Mack, who was dark-headed and slender. If I hadn't met them together, I would have thought Mack was an unlikely father. All the same, he had a natural tone in his voice when he called the boy "son," and when Acie said "Daddy" in his whimpering way, it sounded as if this was the only life these two had ever known.

Except for the circumstance of sharing a quonset hut, Mack and Acie were no more important to me than anyone else in the labor camp. If they spent more time with the family next door than they did in our place, that was all the same with me. No one was going to be friends for very long in this life. But they struck me as interesting all the same. As much by contrast as anything else, they made me think of my own old man.

* * * * *

There was a time, when I was Acie's age and a few years older, that my dad and I knocked around following the crops, living in labor camps and cabin courts when things were going all right and living in the car when they weren't. When we traveled, he would give me two twenty-dollar bills and tell me to put one in each sock. The first time I did it, I put the bills beneath the soles of my feet, inside the socks, but since we were just living in the car, I didn't take my socks off for a couple of days. When I did, fear spread through me as I saw the soft, greenish paper falling apart. Lucky for us, the serial numbers were still legible, so we changed the pieces for new bills. After that, I put money across the tops of my feet.

One day when I was fifteen I got separated from my old man. I was wearing clean socks with a twenty in each one, and I came out of the matinée to wait for him in the bright sun. He didn't show up. I waited outside the theater for four or five hours, getting hungrier and hungrier, but I didn't dare take out one of the bills to get something to eat. I just waited as the hollow feeling set in. Another crowd of people, all strangers, went in to the evening show as I stood on the side-walk. When they were gone, I sat on the curb. Night came on. The cops drove by every once in a while and looked at me. Then when the night was dark and the theater lights were shining and all the bugs were out, a cop stopped and asked me a bunch of questions. He took me down to the station and told me they had my father there. They were going to let him out when he was sober.

Later that year his piss turned brown, dark as coffee, and he went into the hospital for a while. We picked olives, then oranges, and he went into the hospital again. He didn't come out the front door. The car disappeared, and I ended up in a foster home. It was one of a few.

When I moved in with Mack and Acie, then, it got me to remembering things I didn't think about every day. At least my old man had a car, and we both knew how to do our fair share of work, so we did end up with a couple of twenties now and then, even if they didn't last long.

I remembered the year my old man and I picked grapes, after the time he got thrown in jail and before his piss turned brown. We went down to Selma, in the Fresno area, where a contractor set us up in an old farmhouse. We got one bed-room, while a Mexican man and his son got another. They were clean and polite, and the man told us he had a regular job in a shop in Merced. He had two weeks of vacation, so he and his son came down here to make some money for the family. He said he had done this kind of work when he was growing up, and he didn't seem to mind going back to it for a while. Even when a big Mexican family swarmed in and took over the rest of the house, the man from Merced acted as if he was renting a room in a boarding house.

My old man and I didn't like it at all. When the loud radio went off in the morning and the pots and pans started banging, I went and heated a pan of water on the stove, then took it back to our room, where we made instant coffee. For the three weeks we stayed there we ate like we did in the car—bread and jam, Velveeta and soda crackers, bologna and white bread, cold food out of the can. As soon as the sun was up, we were out with our pans and curved knives, cutting grapes to lay on the brown waxed paper in the sun. After we ate in the evening we would go out and pick a few more trays rather than sit around in the house and listen to the racket. The Mexican family had the toilet in their side of the house, so the rest of us went to the rented toilets out in the yard. Even there, one of the Mexican kids would come up and ask questions through the door. Where are you from? How old are you? Have you dropped out of school?

I've lived in a lot of low places, even in a bunkhouse that was just a barn with plywood partitions and no ceiling, but that house at the edge of the long rows of grapevines made me feel more like an animal than any place I've ever stayed. By comparison, the quonset didn't seem bad at all.

* * * * *

While Mack and Acie were at the quonset next door, I unpacked. I had just gotten my few things put away when Mack returned. He had the other man with him, and they walked past me where I was sitting on the couch.

"It's in here," said Mack.

The man followed him to the corner of the kitchen area, where a white wooden box was mounted on the wall. The man opened the door of the box, which was a fuse box as I expected. On the bottom ledge of the box were a couple of round, screw-in fuses. The man picked up a fuse, held it with the flat face towards him, and tilted his head so he could look down through his glasses. Then with his head still tipped, he studied the fuses in the panel. A couple had yellow on the face, and a couple had blue.

"This one looks burned out," he said. He pulled the lever down to cut off the juice, then unscrewed a yellow fuse and put the replacement in. When he flipped the lever up, the refrigerator kicked on and started humming.

"That must be it," said Mack.

"Yeah, not much to it." The man closed the door of the box, and he and Mack came to the front part of the room.

"This is A.D.," said Mack.

I got up from the couch and shook his hand. "My name's Morgan," I said. "Morgan Cross."

The man was about average height and build, starting to go grey. He wore bifocals and a close-fitting khaki cap, the type that had a little pocket in front, right above the beak. He glanced around the interior of the quonset, then came back to me and said, "What do you think of it?"

"It's all right, I guess."

"You get along in this kind of work?" He looked as if he was at home in it, as he wore a loose, long-sleeved grey shirt and khaki pants to go along with his cap.

I had learned from my old man not to knock fruit tramping with people who did it. "Oh, yeah," I said. "I'm used to it. I'd like to move up, of course."

A.D. stood relaxed as he dug out a pack of Chesterfields. "I guess we'd all like to," he said. "But it's a way to get by until we do."

I nodded, and as I did so I caught a glimpse of Mack. Everyone had his own way of getting by, I thought, and anyone who moved up in this life was going to have to figure his own way to do it.

Chapter Two

The orchard was shadowy and cool when I started the day's work. The other pickers had left their buckets hanging on their ladders the day before, but I had to wait until Len brought a ladder and picking bucket for me. Then I went to work. It was not a very noisy place, just the sounds of workers talking back and forth, fruit falling into the metal buckets, and the third leg of a ladder clacking against the steps when someone pulled the ladder up straight and got ready to set it again.

Six of us were picking four rows—Mack and Acie, A.D. and his two sons, and me. When we took a break at ten, the day was beginning to warm up, but the shade of the trees was still comfortable. Mack told Acie and the other two kids to get us some empty lug boxes to sit on, so they put six boxes in kind of a circle. Then Acie stretched out on the ground and let out a long wheeze.

"Tired, Acie?" asked one of the other kids.

"It's just that the bucket gets so heavy."

From the next row over, I had noticed that Acie didn't work on a ladder. He picked bottoms, and he spent a good part of the time with both hands draped on the edge of his picking bucket as he stared away at nothing. He emptied the bucket before it ever got half-full, but still it was evident that the whole prospect was more than he could deal with.

A.D.'s two kids were good workers. They went up and down the ladder and didn't miss a motion. The older one was dark-haired, and the younger one had blondish hair. Now at break time they sat on boxes near their father.

Earlier that morning, I had seen A.D. and the kids waiting in the car for Mack and Acie to come out to ride with them. Now in the orchard I could tell that A.D. had taught his kids that when there was work, you worked, and when you took a break you didn't dick around throwing dirt clods.

Mack rolled a cigarette, and A.D. shook out a Chesterfield. I lit up a Winston. When Mack lit his, he blew away the smoke and wrinkled his nose.

"Len come by and give Acie some shit about pickin' green cots," he said. "I told him the kid was just learnin', and he said he knew that and he was bein' nice to the kid. Someone else, he might fire him. Said if he wanted to, he could fire someone because he didn't like the way he parted his hair."

A.D. leaned forward and rested his arms on his knees. "I've worked for guys like him before. Like the Chinaman says, 'He a plick.'"

His two kids laughed.

"Well," said Mack, "he's the boss and we ain't. But still, pick on a kid that's just learnin'."

A.D. sniffed. "I think they put on too many pickers. Go through too fast, before the fruit can ripen up. I don't know why they do that, but they do. Even on the second time through, there'll be green fruit. You wait and see. Makes it hard to try to do things right and still make a living." He looked at me. "Ain't that right?"

"Yeah," I said. "That's the way it seems." It reminded me of my own old man, who liked to do things right when he could.

"Green as gourds," said Mack. "Isn't that what he said, Acie?"

The kid spoke with a pout as he said, "Yeah."

"Well, fuck him. I don't like him."

I wouldn't have been surprised to find out that Mack didn't like very many people at all.

* * * * *

Later that afternoon, Len came by where I was picking on my row. He was waiting when I came down from my ladder. I had been picking up in the top of the tree, so all of the apricots in my bucket were orange and blushed with red. He looked at them and didn't say anything until I came back from emptying my bucket.

"Pretty good pickin' here."

"It's all right," I said.

"It's pretty damn good, especially at forty cents a box. They're payin' thirty-five for this in all the other places."

I knew that was a lie, but I didn't answer right away. I just looked at him, and I realized why he had seemed familiar when he hired me the day before. He had dark, beady eyes, and the rest of his scowling face reminded me of the front-page newspaper pictures I had seen of Richard Nixon a couple of years earlier when he lost the race for governor. I didn't like this foreman any more than Mack did, but seeing him as

Richard Nixon in a San Francisco Giants ball cap, looking to chew out poor fruit pickers, gave me a way to tolerate him for the time being.

"I'm not complainin'," I said.

"How 'bout the camp? You all right where I put you?"

"Oh, yeah. Everything's fine."

"That's good." He looked around. "Make sure you keep these four rows about even. Someone gets behind, whoever's ahead picks a tree on their row. The others already know that."

"Yeah, they told me." As soon as I said it, I realized I could just as well have let him have the last word on the subject. But he found something more to say anyway.

"Nobody pulls any shit on a crew of mine. Some places, they let a bunch get out ahead of the rest, and then they go pickin' the bottoms of everyone else's trees. Or they skip a bad tree. Shit like that. But they don't do it here." He shook his head and held his beady eyes on me.

"That's good," I said, pleased to give him his own words back.

"You damn right it is." He turned and walked away, so he got in the last word after all.

* * * * *

The way Len had us set out, I took one row, Mack and Acie took one row, and A.D. and his kids took two rows. The lug boxes were stacked on each side of the drive that went between the two middle rows. So we made up one bunch that picked four rows. The four young Mexican guys made up another. They went like hell in the early part of the day, so I didn't see much of them. In the last drive, the Mexican family picked two rows, and the white family picked the other two. I wouldn't have seen much of them that first day except the father came over at about two in the afternoon to bum some matches from A.D.

He didn't seem to be in a hurry to go back to work. He talked to A.D. for a few minutes, then hung around Mack's tree for a few more. After that he stopped to talk to me.

He wore an old straw hat that looked as if it had been run over a few times by a tractor, and he had funny-colored, short hair that was either really light blond or prematurely white. I placed him at about forty. He was lean with a rough complexion and washed-out blue eyes, and he wore a long-sleeved work shirt. As soon as he spoke, I placed him in that general bunch of people who came from Oklahoma, Texas, and Arkansas.

"Naht gonna git rich at this, are we?"

"Probably not," I said.

He shook out a Lucky Strike and lit it. "Len says this fruit's gonna ripen fast." He gave me a squint-eyed look. "I told him, once the pickin' gits better, you'll knock it down a nickel a box. He said he wouldn't, but we'll see. The big boss has the say on that, but I 'magine he listens to Len."

"I guess."

He looked past my ladder. "You're lucky you don't have anyone on the other side of you."

I shrugged.

"You finish these rows before we do, then you'll have them Mexicans next to you. When we come back the other way."

"All the same to me."

He gave me a knowing look. "Maybe you haven't seen much. But they'll come back out here after work, switch ladders on you. They walk their ladder around when they're on it, and they loosen it up. Then they give it to you. They'll steal your pickin' bucket, too."

"Is that right?" I recalled the buckets hanging by their straps on the ladders that morning.

"You damn right. I told Len he should paint numbers on 'em, like they do in other places." He took a drag on his cigarette and narrowed his eyes again. "They don't do it to me, though."

"Uh-huh."

"When me and my boys leave for the day, I put a cigarette paper in the bottom of each one of our buckets. They see that, and they don't put their hands on 'em."

"No shit."

"You damn right." He cocked his head back. "Well, I'd better git back and look after my kids. They start to slow down this time of day."

"I'll see you later, then."

"Sure. By the way, name's Harold."

"Mine's Morgan," I said. "Morgan Cross."

He paused for a second. "Not related to Morgan Hill, are you?"

That was the next main town if you went south on the highway. "No," I said. "Morgan's my first name. My last name's Cross."

"Well, mine's Hubbs. Harold Hubbs."

"Good enough."

As he walked away, I wondered how he might think I was related to Morgan Hill. From the way he had said it, it seemed as if he thought the town was named after a person's first and last name, which would mean he had the notion that people were related through their first names. I shook my head. Then I pondered the logic of the cigarette paper, shook my head again, and went back to work.

* * * * *

Our group made the turn at the end of the orchard the next day, just before Hubbs and the rest of that group did, so the Mexican family ended up on my left as Hubbs said they might. I didn't mind it, though. There was a kid about sixteen or seventeen, and when he found out I spoke Spanish, we got along like old friends. On top of that, he had a sister who was a year or so older. It was the girl I had seen the first day. She kept herself wrapped up like Mexican girls do, to keep from getting darker and showing that they worked in the fields. She wore long pants, a long-sleeved shirt, gloves, and a scarf that covered her head and the sides of her face. I had already seen her without the scarf, and I was sure that underneath the bundling she was a nice-looking girl. Her brother called her Rosy, with a hard s, short for Rosa María as I found out. I thought

104

the full name was a pretty one, and it reminded me of the desert rose you hear about, the kind that blooms in a place where no one ever sees it.

The brother's name was Francisco, and then there was the father and a couple of younger kids as well. No one under sixteen was supposed to go above the red line painted at the five-foot step on the ladder, but these kids went right on up. Len never said a word about it that I knew, not to them or to Hubbs or A.D.

The family's last name was Carrillo. They were nice people, and I couldn't imagine them scheming on my ladder or picking bucket. Of course, there were plenty others who would— Mexicans or Okies or you name it.

By the time the Carrillos made the turn and came up working alongside me, I had a count on who was working in which group. I realized that Rosa María was the only girl in the orchard. When she went to the bathroom, she had to go all the way to the end where the portable toilets were, so she took one of the younger boys with her.

By the third day, I got to wondering where the colored man and the white woman were working. I had seen them in the labor camp in the morning and evening, and I had seen their Tokay bottles in the trash barrel out back. They were an unusual couple, I thought. He was very dark, and she was light and brown-haired with a big purple birthmark on the left side of her face and neck. They had an old Black Dodge, a '52 or '53, with the ram's head ornament on the hood.

That afternoon, on the third day, I found out where they were working. It came up in conversation when Hubbs and his two kids came over to join our bunch for an afternoon break.

Hubbs was going on about how his kids got all ones and twos "baick East," where the schools were harder and of course better. I didn't care for the two kids and the way they skulked and glared, so I didn't look at them when their father was singing their praises.

I thought A.D. was playing along when he said, "Is that right?" Then he said, "Well, here's what Mike did." He pulled out his wallet and unfolded a piece of paper, the kind that would have had carbon copies underneath. He held it out for each of us to see. It was a report card with Michael Ashburn's name on it, and the kid had gotten all A's.

Hubbs barely glanced at it, and his two kids ignored it, just as Acie did. None of them struck me as compulsive readers. Mike looked embarrassed, so I changed the subject.

"Say, where's that couple in the black Dodge? I don't see them anywhere out here."

Hubbs answered. "Len's got them in another orchard. The other camp's full, so he put 'em with us. Can't say that I care for it."

Mack's eyes came up from rolling a cigarette. "What's wrong with it?"

Hubbs tipped his ashes and said, "Well, in some places they've got laws about people shackin' up like that."

"Bah," said Mack. "Who the hell's business is it, what a man and a woman do?"

"I'm not just talkin' about a man and a woman." The white straw hat wagged back and forth as Hubbs lifted his cigarette and held it near his chin. "I'm talkin' about a nigger and a white woman."

"Ah, shit," said Mack. "What the hell's the difference?"

Hubbs got a tight look. "Where I come from, there is."

"Then you come from a different part of the country than I do. White woman wants to screw a colored man, it's no different than a white man wantin' to screw a colored girl. That right, A.D.?"

"I s'pose."

Hubbs wasn't giving up. "Well," he said, "they'd better not do it in some places, unless they want to go to jail."

"They do it everywhere," said Mack. "That and worse. I was in the service, and I know."

"Maybe so," said A.D., "but these kids don't need to know about it. Not yet."

Mack lit his cigarette. "Wise 'em up. Teach 'em to stay away from punks."

"You mean pachucos?" asked Hubbs.

Mack's eyes blazed. "I mean punks. A punk is a man that gets fucked in the ass."

No one said anything. After a long, uncomfortable moment, A.D. said, "I didn't know Len had two crews."

"Sure," said Hubbs. "That's why he comes and goes."

* * * * *

That evening, Francisco invited me to eat with his family.

His mother had made up a kind of a stew, with hamburger and bell peppers and tomatoes and onions, plus a few noodles. She served from a pot on the stove, and when I finished my first bowl she gave me a second helping. I enjoyed the meal and the company, though not everyone ate at once. The mother and the girl waited until the rest of us were done, and then they sat down at the other end of the table. Rosa María looked different than she did in the field, opened up and clean and shiny, but she still kept her distance. When I spoke to her in Spanish, she answered in English. I didn't blame her. I knew it was rough being a pretty girl when your family followed the crops and lived in labor camps.

On my way out the door, I saw Hubbs sitting on his doorstep. He waved me over, so I made a small detour to see what he wanted.

After we each said good evening, he gave me a confidential look and said, "Don't take Mack too serious."

"In what way?"

"Oh, he gets hotter'n a pistol. I can see that. And since you're livin' in the same place as him, I was hopin' he didn't aggravate you too much."

"Oh, no," I said. "He hasn't bothered me a bit."

At that moment, someone appeared in the open doorway. It was a woman with mouse-colored hair. I remembered seeing her the first day. She said a couple of words to Hubbs, and he reached into his shirt pocket and held up a pack of Luckies. As she took it, I got a look at her. She wore a sleeveless dress that went straight down all the way around, and I could see she had held her age better than her husband had.

She took a cigarette from the pack, and as she handed it back to the man, she turned her eyes on me and said, "Hi." She seemed to take me in with a full look as I said "Hi" back to her. Then she went into the house.

Hubbs picked up the thread of conversation from before. "Anyway, if he gives you any trouble, just tell Len."

"Sure. But I don't expect any at all." I glanced over at the quonset and said, "Well, I guess I'll go back. We'll see you tomorrow."

"Yep. We'll be back at it again."

As I walked across the hard-packed road, the image of Mrs. Hubbs flickered through my mind. From there I thought about her husband's advice for me not to take Mack's comments too seriously, and I wondered which ones he might have meant. Then I wondered what he thought of me eating dinner with the Carrillo family, after he had been so thoughtful as to warn me about their kind.

Chapter Three

The colored man and the white woman moved out the next day, and two guys in their late twenties moved into that half of the quonset. I recognized them as the two swampers, guys who set out empty boxes ahead of us and picked up the full ones we left behind. They started later than the pickers, at about 8:00, and they worked later in the day to get out all the fruit. I hadn't paid them much mind, but now they were in the camp, so I met them.

That evening they stood out in front of the two quonsets, where they looked over the rest of the camp and talked in loud voices as they smoked their cigarettes. They both wore shirts with the sleeves cut away, like they were hay haulers. One of them was tall and dark-headed, and he wore his hair slicked back and up and over, like he was Elvis Presley or Fabian. The other one was of average height, thick in the neck and shoulders, with a red complexion that rose in shiny welts. He had dry, brown hair that he parted on one side.

When I went out to sit on the front steps, they came over to talk to me. The tall one said his name was Fletcher, and the other one introduced himself as Bernie.

Fletcher said they had just moved in. Len had an opening in his other camp, so the man and woman went there. "I guess he was a nigger," he said.

"Probably still is," said Bernie.

I didn't say anything.

"You makin' any kind of money?" Fletcher asked.

"Not much. I make about twelve, fourteen dollars a day."

"Yeah, none of this pays worth a shit," he said. "We get enough to travel on, we're gonna go back to the oilfields."

"How does that pay?"

He closed his eyes halfway as he took a drag on his cigarette. "About fifty bucks a day."

"How do you get into that line of work?"

"You just do it."

"You mean, you go up to 'em and say you're a roughneck?"

"Roustabout," said Bernie.

"And how do you know how to do the work if they hire you?"

"You just fuckin' do it," said Fletcher. He snapped his cigarette butt away.

"I wouldn't know what to do."

"You go with us, we'll get you on," said Bernie.

"It's an idea."

Bernie lifted his elbow high in the air as he took a drag on his cigarette, then tipped his head back as he blew out the smoke. "Beats the shit out of this. You make more in a week there than you make in a month here."

"Where do you go for work like that?"

"All over," said Fletcher."Bakersfield, Ventura, Oxnard."

"Work year-round?"

Bernie dropped his cigarette and stepped on it. "You work as much as you want."

I looked from one to the other as I considered what that might mean.

* * * * *

I was standing in the front room of the quonset hut after work the next day, just gazing out the window, when A.D.'s son Mike came up the wooden steps and knocked on the door. When I opened, he told me his dad sent him over to invite me to eat dinner with them. Mack and Acie were already there, he said. I figured these people didn't waste any time getting a meal on the table, so I said I'd be over right away.

Mack and Acie were there, all right, still in their work clothes. They hadn't come back to our quonset at all, so I assumed they'd gone straight into A.D.'s place when the car pulled in.

Mack was sitting across the table from A.D., with a gallon of Italian Swiss Colony muscatel between them. Each of them had a water glass half-full of the yellowish stuff. I had seen an empty half-pint Ten High bottle underneath the sink at our place, so I took Mack for a whiskey drinker. Now when I saw him drinking A.D.'s wine, I imagined he was out of Ten High.

Acie was sitting on an old couch with A.D.'s two kids. Mike asked me if I wanted to play hangman, and I said, "Not right now."

A.D. pointed at the jug of muscatel. "Want a glass of wine?" he asked.

"Not yet, thanks."

At the other end of the big room, just like in our quonset, sat a kitchen area. A red-haired woman with her back to me was stirring a big speckled enamel pot, and steam was rising.

"Sit down," said A.D.

I took a seat next to Mack, not too far from where the kids sat on the couch.

"Sure you don't want a drink?"

"I'll wait till I eat something."

The woman set a large yellow salad bowl on the table. "Hi," she said. "I'm Marge."

I introduced myself, and she went back to the kitchen area. A minute later, she reappeared and set a smaller bowl and an armful of ingredients on the table. She scooped a couple of big gobs of mayonnaise into the bowl, then pounded on the bottom of a ketchup bottle until half a cup spilled out. After that she poured in some brown vinegar and stirred the mixture with the mayonnaise spoon.

"Mike," she said. "Come over and do the salad dressing so I can go back to the spaghetti."

The kid stirred up the mess and scraped it into the larger bowl on top of the chopped lettuce and celery and onions. Then he went back to the couch.

He and his brother were trying to teach Acie to play hangman, and I had a pretty good idea of who was going to get hanged first. Mike was making up the page, and he asked Acie how to spell his name.

"A-S-A."

"What's that?"

"That's my name."

"But everyone calls you Acie. How do you spell that?"

"I don't know."

"Well, what do you put on your papers at school?"

"I don't know. I don't hardly ever go."

"Oh. Well, how about A-C-I-E?"

"I guess so. Is that right, Daddy?"

"Sure it is, son. You know that." Mack looked at the other two kids. "Don't make fun of him, now."

"We're not," said Mike. "We're just teachin' him a game."

A.D. spoke up. "Why don't you play the game later? Help Marge set the table."

Mike heaved a breath and got up from the couch. He brought a stack of plates from the kitchen, and as he set them out, A.D. pushed the ashtray aside and lowered the gallon of muscatel to the floor. Mike came back with silverware and a stack of brown plastic cereal bowls. Marge laid two hot pads in the middle of the table, and a minute later she set down the steaming pot of spaghetti.

I began to wonder where everyone was going to sit until A.D. said, "You kids serve yourselves first, and you can eat on the couch."

"Here's bread and butter," said Marge. She laid a loaf of Wonder bread on the table, then took a stick of margarine out of a pack, unwrapped it, and put it on a saucer.

The big yellow bowl went around, and as each person finished his salad, Marge spooned out spaghetti onto a plate from the stack. It was simple but not bad—just boiled spaghetti,

114

tomato sauce, and bland hamburger. About half the loaf of Wonder bread disappeared along with it.

When the meal was done, Mike and his brother Steve washed all the dishes. Marge poured herself a glass of wine, lit a cigarette, and started a game of solitaire. She didn't pay much attention to the two boys, but when they were done with the dishes, A.D. told them to make the sandwiches for the next day. I divided my attention between watching Mike twist the key on the Spam can and Marge shuffle the cards for her next hand.

She looked over at me. "Do you play cards?"

"Not much. I was just watching you shuffle."

"I was married to a card player once. I guess some of it rubbed off."

"I see."

"He used to sit at the kitchen table and practice at night. Shufflin' and dealin'. I could hear him from the bedroom, and when I heard a card flap, I'd say, 'Johnny, you're slippin'.'"

"You mean he dealt—"

"Yeah, any way he wanted."

"Huh."

She lit another cigarette and dealt out the cards in their columns.

I turned back to be part of A.D. and Mack's company. They talked about work—what kind there was, and where you could find it. Mack said it was just as well for him and Acie to work together rather than get a job by himself and have to wonder what the kid was gettin' into during the day. A.D.

said that was right, it didn't hurt these kids a damn bit to work. Marge kept to her solitaire game and didn't comment.

I didn't want to drink any more than my one glass of wine, so I just sat there. Acie was sitting by himself, moping on the couch, but I couldn't think of anything to talk to him about. After a while the other two kids came back, and Mike asked me if I wanted to play rummy. I said no, thanks. Then it occurred to me that I could say something polite.

"That was a nice report card you got," I said.

"Oh, yeah. I don't expect anyone to believe it, though."

Mack spoke up. "Acie, why don't you run next door and bring me back a sack of Bull Durham?"

The kid's whiny voice came from the couch. "Aw, Daddy, do I have to?"

"Here, Mack," said Marge, "Have one of mine."

"Nah, I don't want to smoke all of yours, and it won't hurt this kid to go. One of these others can go with him."

"Mike," said A.D.

I saw my opening, so I got up and stretched. "It's probably about time for me to go, too, so they can both go over with me. I thank you all for the meal."

"You're welcome," said Marge without looking up.

"Any time," said A.D. "We'll see you in the morning."

It was getting dark outside when I went down the steps of their quonset with the two kids behind me. I looked to see if I could catch a glance of Rosa María, but no one was outside at the Carrillo house. Past it, Mrs. Hubbs was sitting on the doorstep where her husband sometimes sat. She was smoking a cigarette, and she looked my way as I went up the steps to my own place. A few minutes later when I looked out the window, she was still there, but the next time I looked, she had gone inside like everyone else.

* * * * *

I began to feel like a regular dinner guest when Francisco invited me to his family's house for a second time. Life was so dull around the labor camp that I would have appreciated the variety even if he didn't have a good-looking sister. So I cleaned up and went over there after I came in from the field.

This time the pot on the stove had turkey legs cooked in a thin chile sauce, the kind they call *biria*. I had seen goat and cow heads cooked in sauce like that, and it was all good. After Francisco's mother served me a turkey leg, rice, and beans, she showed me a stack of corn tortillas wrapped in a dish towel. The father had already started to eat, so when I was served, I dug in as well.

Rosa María looked clean and bright as before, but she kept to the kitchen and didn't say anything to me. When I finished eating and left the table, she came out of the kitchen with a plate of food and sat at the other end. Francisco asked if I wanted to go outside and walk around, so I said all right.

We walked down to the corner where the road from the highway turned a sharp right and headed into the camp. The tree frogs and crickets were chirping, and from time to time one of the huge bugs of the night went whirring by.

Francisco liked to talk, so he went on and on. He said they had come from a town called Monclova in northern Mexico. They worked in the onions and the peppers in Texas and first came to Gilroy to work in the garlic. Then when more of them were big enough to work on ladders, they came back to pick apricots and then pears or peaches. The peaches were a long ways away, so they might not go there this year. This same company had pears, and the boss said they wouldn't have to move camps if they stayed for the pear season.

Francisco said that with the money they made here, they could go back and spend the winter in Texas, where they rented a house for ten dollars a month. His father worked in the winter, but the kids didn't. They liked it in Texas because it didn't get cold. And meat was cheaper, especially if they bought it in Piedras Negras. That was across the border from Eagle Pass. His mother liked it there in Texas. Everyone spoke Spanish. And they could go visit the family in Coahuila. No one wanted to go back to live in Monclova, though. There were no bathrooms in the houses, and too many people still went around with horses and wagons. Everyone had cars here, and televisions. They had a television, but they left it in the house in Eagle Pass. He might get a job this winter. He was old enough.

I asked him if he went to school, and he said not any more. I asked him if his sister went to school. She went until she was eighteen, he said. I asked if she had any boyfriends, and he laughed and said he didn't know. If she did, she wouldn't let him or his father know about it. But he didn't think she did. She didn't like anyone, as far as he could tell.

When we went back to his house, Rosa María was throwing a brown-orange soccer ball back and forth with the two younger kids. When the ball hit the ground and rolled away, Francisco went after it, blocked it, and came back dribbling it with his feet. For the next several minutes, he kicked the ball back and forth with his two little brothers.

I took advantage of the chance to talk to Rosa María. I said, "Your brother tells me your family might work here in the pears."

"That's what my father wants."

The sun had gone down beyond the mountains on the far side of the orchard, and dusk was drawing in. Her face was not as bright as it had been earlier, but her light brown complexion was still clear and soft, with no blemishes. Her dark eyes and eyelashes held my attention. I had not been this close to a Mexican girl before, and I was surprised at how real she became.

"What do *you* want?" I asked.

"Me?" she said. "To stay or go? It doesn't matter. I just want the summer to be over, with no more working in the fields." Then she surprised me by asking, "And you, what do you want?"

"For right now, I want to make a living."

"And that's all," she said.

"Well, not really. I mean, you have things you want for right now, and then there's the things you want more . . . eventually, I guess."

She didn't look straight at me but gazed out across the top of the orchard. "So what do you want, after the apricots and the pears?"

When someone asked me what my plan or goal was, I had a ready answer. I would say it was to stay out of jail. It was my way of saying that when you were living hand-to-mouth, it was kind of silly to say what you wanted in the long run. But I felt I should give her a serious answer, so I said, "I guess what I want is to move up a notch in the world, or at least keep from getting stuck where I am, and I want to do it without doing things that I wouldn't be proud of later." I thought the last part sounded kind of vague, so I added, "Like lying or cheating or stealing—or just trying to get favors."

"So you want to move up?"

"Doesn't everyone?"

She waved her arm at the labor camp. "See for yourself. Doesn't it seem to you that some people are satisfied with where they are?"

"I don't know. I just assumed everyone wanted to do better."

"Maybe they do. But I think some people want to be where they are, or they don't want to change bad enough to give up their ways."

I thought of Mack drinking A.D.'s muscatel while Marge played solitaire. I wondered if Rosa María meant them, the two swampers who had just moved in, the four young Mexican guys, the Hubbs family, or everyone in general. From the way she had waved her arm, I didn't think she referred to her own family, but she may have meant them as well. She was a pretty girl in a dismal way of life, and I could tell that her pride had given her a hard shell.

At that moment, the two Hubbs kids went strolling by, not far from where Francisco was standing and waiting for the ball.

One of the kids passed a remark, and Francisco whipped around fast enough to make them both jump back. Francisco had his fists at his sides, and he barked at them in English with a heavy accent.

"You're gonna get your ass kicked."

The older kid, whose name was Dean, said, "Aw, go to hell."

"I don't like what you said."

"So what?" Dean raised his chin. He had slicked-back blond hair, blue eyes with dark lower eyelids, and a nose that turned up enough that his nostrils looked like two dark holes in a ditchbank. He wore a t-shirt with the sleeves folded up like he might have seen in a hoodlum movie. Or on other hoodlums. Just the way he stood there made an open invitation for someone to hit him.

"That's my sister."

"Your seester."

Rosa María turned away and went into the house. I felt my stomach tighten, and I wanted to smack the smart-ass, but I made myself stay where I was. This was kid stuff, the two of them sixteen or seventeen years old. I was twenty-two going on twenty-three, and fighting with a kid that age was just one more way to get into trouble.

"That's right," said Francisco. "I heard what you said."

"And what did I say?" Dean raised his chin again, and his burr-headed brother looked like he was ready to jump in as soon as something got started.

"You said she thought she was hot stuff."

Dean wagged his head. "What I said was, I wondered why she thought she was such hot stuff."

If it was possible to make someone want to hit him even more than before, he did it.

"Come on, Francisco," I said in English. "They're just lookin' for trouble. You don't need it."

As Francisco turned to walk away, Dean called in a mocking tone, "Yeah, yeah. You goan to get chore ass keeked."

I shook my head at Francisco and said in Spanish, "Let him go to hell. He's a jerk." Actually I said *pendejo*, which can mean a lot of things, from dumb-ass to fuckhead.

"*Puro pendejo*," he said, in agreement.

He went into the house, and I went back to mine. I felt I had used good judgment in not getting mixed up in a stupid squabble, but deep down, I despised that kid for what he said and what he meant by it. He was like his old man. A person who was anything but white was less than a human. It made me madder than was good for me, and I knew I resented the kid all the more because he had made the remark about a girl I liked.

She had asked me what I wanted. If anybody had asked me now, as I looked out the window of the quonset hut, I might have said it straight out. I wanted to rub that snotty kid's face in the dirt.

Chapter Four

Len brought around the checks on Friday, just before quitting time. The company paid through Wednesday, which was common. Holding back a couple of days' wages was supposed to keep people from pulling out with no warning, and I imagine it gave some people the feeling that they had a little in reserve and hadn't spent every last cent as soon as they made it.

Still, it didn't keep people like Mack from getting payday drunk. As soon as we got back to the camp after work, he and A.D. and Marge went into town. They came back with a load of groceries and other supplies, and I saw that Mack had gotten a carton of Camels and a fifth of Ten High. He took the bottle over to A.D.'s, and I guess he didn't come back until pretty late, because he and Acie stayed home from work the next day.

He didn't look like too much of a wreck that evening, but the empty Ten High bottle was under the sink. As I was getting out of my work clothes, A.D.'s son Mike came over and invited us all to their place for dinner.

By the time I got cleaned up and made it there, Mack was sipping on a glass of A.D.'s muscatel. Red-haired Marge was mixing up a pot of beans, squinting and holding her head to one side as she smoked her cigarette. Mike was managing the can opener, and I could see he had poured in four big cans of kidney beans and half a dozen smaller ones of tomato sauce.

He set down the opener and began putting a tomato sauce can inside each of the empty bean cans. Steve and Acie were sitting on the couch playing tic-tac-toe.

Marge asked me if I'd like a beer, and I said sure. She handed me a can of Pabst and opened one for herself. She went back to stirring the pot, and I drank on my beer.

Mack's voice sounded a little rougher than usual as he told A.D. a bit of gossip. "Good ol' Len came by twice today. Didn't stop to say shit to me, but he parked in front of Hubbs's shack, and the woman came out each time and talked to him for damn near half an hour."

A.D. wrinkled his nose and said, "Yeah, Marge told me the same thing. I guess he comes by just about every day."

"And here's Hubbs, kissin' Len's ass ever' time he comes through the orchard. I wonder if he'd do it as much if he knew what Len was after."

"No tellin'. There's ass-kissers everywhere you go, just like there's people lookin' for nookie. If they stay out of my bidness, I stay out of theirs."

Mack opened his yellow eyes as he took a drag on his cigarette. "Well, they damn sho' stay out of mine. I thought Len might knock on the door, but he let me be. As for Hubbs, I wouldn't tell him a thing, even if someone was screwin' his old lady in broad daylight."

Marge whacked the stirring spoon on the lip of the enamel pot. "This stuff's ready," she said.

A.D. looked up and around. "No salad tonight?"

"I didn't have time," she said. "We'll have some tomorrow." She set the big pot on two hot pads, then came back with the Wonder bread and the margarine as Mike laid out bowls and silverware.

After dinner, I saw that it was Steve's job to take out the trash. He put all the cans in a big brown paper sack and went out the back door. A minute later he showed up with the bag by itself. He put an empty gallon wine jug in it and bunched the paper up around the top. Then he took a hammer from a kitchen drawer and went outside again. I heard a faint *plink*, and Steve came back in with the hammer and put it away.

He and his brother went about washing the dishes, and Marge sat down to deal herself a hand of solitaire. She offered me another beer, and I said no, thanks. Then she told Steve to bring her one, which he did. It looked as if things were settling in for the evening, so I stood up, thanked A.D. and Marge for the meal, and said good-night.

Dusk was closing in as I went back to my quonset. The lights were on in the Carrillo and Hubbs houses, but no one was in view. I went into the dark quonset, turned on a light, and stretched out on my bed. I could hear Mexican music from the other half, and the young guys sounded happy as they talked and laughed. I tried to relax, but it seemed like work just to try to take it easy, not go anywhere on a Saturday night, not have any fun. It was tempting to think that one night wouldn't make a difference, and I had to bear down on myself and remember that when a guy let loose, he usually didn't find anything. After a night of sloshy beer, cigarette smoke, and jukebox music, all a guy had was a hangover and a sense that he needed to get straightened out again. I told myself that every night I stayed home, I was working on moving up a notch. I had my doubts about whether it was true, but on nights like this it kept me from going out and pissing away what little I had.

* * * * *

Everyone else knocked off at about two the next day, so I did too. Actually, Hubbs didn't knock off then because he didn't show up that day. His two sulky kids did, and Mack got it out of them that their old man had gotten too drunk the night before. The one named Dean was old enough to drive, so he was master of the family car for the day. It was a 1956 Ford station wagon with loud mufflers, and the kid liked to rev up the motor and let the mufflers blast.

Back at the labor camp, it looked as if the rest of Sunday afternoon was going to be quiet. The four young Mexican guys in the other half of the quonset got shined up and said they were going to a dance. Mack and Acie went over to A.D.'s, and everyone else kept inside as well. I decided to wash some socks by hand and enjoy the silence. As I was running the water in the sink and wondering what the Mexican dance might be like, I heard a knock at the door. I walked across the room, listening for a voice, but I didn't hear anything.

When I opened the door, I was surprised to see Mrs. Hubbs standing in the doorway.

"Oh, hi," I said. "What can I do for you?"

Her eyes met mine and then drifted. "I'm out of ciga-rettes," she said. "Harold's been on a drunk, and between him and the kids, they've smoked up everything."

"Do you want more than one, then?"

"If you could loan me four or five, I'd appreciate it."

"Okay," I said. "I'll be right back." I left her standing there as I went to my room and got a pack of Winstons.

When I came back, I got a full look at her. She had her hair combed, and she was wearing a pale-yellow, straight, sleeveless dress. She had light-colored eyes, a bluish-grey, and for the moment she seemed much more likeable than the rest of her family. In my drifting thoughts, I figured her for about fifteen years older than me.

I held out the pack of Winstons. "Go ahead and take these," I said. "Maybe they'll keep you until someone goes to town."

"I don't want to take all your cigarettes."

"It's all right. I've got plenty." I handed her the pack, and she took it.

"Thanks." Her face and her shoulders relaxed. "By the way, my name's Blanche."

"Mine's Morgan. Glad to meet you."

She pulled the thin band off the cellophane and peeled away the wrapper, then opened the flip-top and pulled out a cigarette. "Can I get a light?" she asked.

I struck a match and held it for her.

She turned her head to blow away the smoke, and then she let out a weary breath. "Jesus," she said, "I'm glad to get out of that house for a few minutes. When he gets drunk like that, he just lays in bed and hollers out at everyone else to do this, do that. Wears out my patience."

"Yeah, I know. It's not fun to put up with."

She took another puff. Her eyes met mine for an instant and slid away. "Well, I don't need to tell you all my troubles, make you listen to things you've heard before."

"It's all right. It doesn't bother me."

"Well, thanks. And thanks for the cigarettes. I'll pay you back."

"Don't worry about it."

"I'll get you a full pack."

"If you get a chance, that's fine."

"Thanks." She turned away and went down the steps. As she headed towards her house, she tossed the cellophane wrapper aside.

Life in a labor camp was empty enough that a woman like her was interesting for a moment, but I didn't want her to look back and see me watching her, so I closed the door and went to run some more hot water in the sink.

I was wringing out my socks for a last time when I heard noise in front. I went to the window and looked out to see the two swampers. The tall, dark-haired one named Fletcher had just settled in behind the steering wheel of their green Oldsmobile, and he was rolling down the window. His pal Bernie was standing in front of my doorstep calling out.

I opened the door.

"Hey," said Bernie. "We're going into town. You wanna go?"

"I guess so."

I set the two pair of socks on the back of a chair to dry, grabbed my cigarettes, and went outside. Bernie was sitting on the passenger side of the front seat, and Fletcher was sending blue smoke out the tailpipe as he hit the gas, let off, hit the gas, let off.

The car was a four-door, so I got into the back seat without bothering anyone. Fletcher, with a cigarette drooping from his mouth, backed the Oldsmobile out onto the rutted road. He looked at me in the rear-view mirror.

"What did Hubbs's old lady want?"

I thought he was being forward, but I let it pass. "She was out of cigarettes," I said.

"I would've given her some."

"I bet you would," said Bernie.

Fletcher stepped on it and boiled up a cloud of dust.

"You might let up," I said. "These guys with orchards don't like a lot of dust settlin' on their fruit."

"It's Sunday," he said. "There's no one around." He slowed, hung a left, and stepped on it again as we headed for the highway.

I expected Len to show up at any second as we passed the drying yard and went on with orchards on both sides.

Fletcher turned left at the highway and went into Morgan Hill, where he found a liquor store soon enough.

"You want anything?" he asked.

"No, not now," I said.

They went into the store and puttered around for a while, then came out each with a bottle of Squirt.

Back on the highway, Fletcher shifted in his seat and pulled out a pint of Jim Beam.

"Well, son of a bitch," said Bernie. "You did get something."

"They were givin' it away." Fletcher twisted off the cap, took a slug of whiskey, handed the bottle to his partner, and chased the Jim Beam with a drink of Squirt.

Bernie did the same, with a bottle in each hand, and then he turned to me. "You want some?"

"No, thanks," I said.

"You sure?"

"Yeah."

Bernie shrugged and handed the pint to Fletcher, who looked at me again in the mirror.

"I bet you can fuck her," he said.

I frowned. "How's that?"

"The one you gave the cigarettes to."

"I'm not too interested." I could smell the whiskey now, and it was tempting, but I didn't like anything about those two guys, and I didn't want to share their stolen liquor.

"Well, I think it can be done." He tipped up the Jim Beam, took a drink, and lowered the bottle. He drove on as if he was thinking of something to add, but he didn't say anything. He handed the whiskey to his pal and took a gulp of Squirt.

"You know what they say," said Bernie. "It's all good. Just some of it's better."

I braced myself and waited to see if either of them was going to make a crack about anyone else in the labor camp, but it must not have occurred to them. That was fine with me.

* * * * *

Francisco knocked on my door at about six the next evening. In his rapid-fire way of talking, he told me there were some *señores* who came to sell things, and I should come and take a look. I had just finishing eating, so I left my dirty dishes on the table and went with him across the road.

I saw a shiny, white 1960 Ford parked between the Carrillo house and the Hubbs house. A man was standing by the driver's door, talking to Francisco's father. The visitor wore a white straw hat, a white shirt, and black Frisco jeans. As I got closer, I saw that he had a trimmed mustache and a clean shave. Another man, who was dressed and groomed the same way, appeared from the other side of the car. He went around the back end, stopped, and opened the trunk.

From a few yards away, I could see they had merchandise for sale. Stacked in the trunk were flats of canned sodas, cartons of cigarettes, bars of bath soap, and packages of frosted cinnamon rolls, with a few transistor radios sitting on top of the sodas and cigarettes. I recognized the type of vendors these guys were, and I imagined they had smaller items as well—things like cigarette lighters, pocket knives, and wrist watches. I had seen fellows like them in other labor camps, especially where there were a lot of braceros who didn't see some of this stuff in Mexico and who didn't get to town very often. These guys were bootleggers, nothing very serious.

The man talking to Francisco's father fit the type to a *T*. He was soft with a shiny bronze complexion and small dark eyes, and he wore a turquoise ring as well as a watch with a wide chrome wristband. The man who opened the trunk had larger eyes, a darker and coarser complexion, and a thicker mustache. His hands looked rougher and he wore no rings, just a wristwatch.

Francisco walked up to the trunk of the car and asked the man about a radio. Right away the fellow turned on a black radio, pulled out the antenna, and dialed in a Mexican station. The music was loud, and I didn't hear all the chatter between Francisco and the salesman. I wasn't much interested in any of the stuff that was for sale, so I let my attention drift back to the other man.

He had a distracted look on his face. Rosa María had just walked out onto the doorstep, and the man, who was carrying on a matter-of-fact conversation with her father, seemed to be absorbed by her appearance. I could tell he was making an effort to look at her father and keep up the conversation, but his dark eyes kept drifting back to the girl.

The other man's voice saved me from staring. He spoke to me in English. "Hey, boy, what you want? You wanna buy a watch?"

"No, thanks," I said. "I'm not looking for anything."

"How 'bout one of these?" He held up a round shaving mirror, the kind with wire brackets for a stand.

"No, thanks," I said again.

He turned the volume down on the radio. "We gotta lotta stuff. Take a look."

I was about to say "No" for the third time when Harold Hubbs's voice cut in.

"Ah'd like to bah one of them radios if I had a little more caish."

"Save your money for a week. We're gonna come back. You need some cigarettes?"

"Not rat now."

"Well, take a look. Maybe you see something else you like."

"Oh, I always see somethin' I like. It's just a matter of havin' the moolah for it. You know?"

"Oh, sure. Too much work, not enough money." He turned to Francisco and spoke in Spanish. "And this other gringo, the young one, does he have any money?"

Francisco said "I don't know" about as quick as a person could.

Hubbs drifted away, but Francisco hung on. He turned the dial to see what other stations he could tune in. He went through the Giants game and stopped at another Mexican station.

The man at the back of the car spoke up in English. "Hey, you. Come and take a look. We gotta lotta stuff."

Fletcher and Bernie were coming across the road, both of them in cutaway shirts and clean Levi's. When they stopped, Fletcher took out a cigarette and lighter, and with a little show of muscle he rapped the cigarette on his lighter before he lit up.

"You wanna buy a watch?"

Fletcher raised his head and blew away the smoke. Then he turned down his mouth as he looked over the merchandise in the open trunk. "Nah," he said.

The man looked past Fletcher. "How 'bout you? Something else?"

Bernie had hooked his thumbs in his front pants pockets. "No dinero," he said.

The two of them sauntered on toward Hubbs's shack.

Francisco fiddled with the radio again, caught Buck Owens as clear as day for about two seconds, and found another Mexican station.

I patted him on the shoulder and said in Spanish, "Good night, Francisco. See you tomorrow."

The salesman gave me a full look and turned his attention back to Francisco.

As I walked away, I cast a glance at the front step and saw that Rosa María had gone inside. Her father was still talking to the pudgy bootlegger, who stood in a slouch as he smoked a cigarette and nodded. They could be talking about a sack of potatoes for all I knew, but I didn't forget the expression on the man's face when he first laid eyes on Rosa María.

Chapter Five

We finished the apricot season with a little bit of chaos. The whole crew had moved through the orchard at a fast pace for the second picking, and the end came in the early afternoon of a Thursday. Rather than have each group knock off when it finished its four rows, Len had the four young Mexican guys and then our bunch work back to meet the Hubbs and Carrillo group. Hubbs had stayed home drunk again that day, so his kids had lagged behind the Mexican family. Our two groups were making uneven progress along the four return rows, and at the finish, everyone met and crossed into one another's rows in the middle of the orchard. The four young Mexicans met up with the Carrillos, then moved over in front of our bunch and marched on the two Hubbs kids. At the very end, two or three people were picking on the same tree, everyone trying to get as much as he could for himself, except for Acie, who took off his picking bucket and sat alone in the shade of a picked tree.

Len came by at about the time the happy young Mexican guys were swarming on the last two trees that the Hubbs kids had grabbed. When the trees were stripped, Len told the kids to go get their father's ladder and bucket, bring them back, and wait. He had some more work for them. Then he told the rest of us to go back to the camp, and he would bring the checks by later in the day.

As I turned to go, he said he had a job for me if I wanted to work by the hour for the rest of the day.

"Sure," I said. "That'll be all right. What kind of work is it?"

"Bankin' out." He waved a hand at the stacked lug boxes. "You and me'll do it. I had these other two guys, but just the tall one showed up this mornin', hung over, and he said his friend was in too bad a shape to even come. I fired the two of 'em. I get tired of worthless sons a bitches that can't stay sober."

It looked as if I was going to fill in for the two swampers. I had noticed that when they hauled the lug boxes out of the orchard, they usually took turns, one driving the tractor and the other loading the boxes onto the trailer. I imagined I was going to do all the stacking and that was why Len picked me rather than any of the younger kids or older men. And besides, I was by myself and he needed only one swamper if he was going to drive the tractor.

I went with him to his pickup and then to the drying yard. I could see the girls working in the shade of the roofed, open area, but I didn't have much time to gawk. Len drove straight to the old red tractor where it was parked at the edge of the asphalt.

Being an orchard tractor, it was a low-slung affair with the seat down between the fenders. Nothing stuck up higher than the radiator cap, not even the steering wheel, and the exhaust pipe went out to the side. I had been around tractors like it before, beasts that were older than I was, so I knew it was a crank-up model with a hand throttle and hand clutch.

Len parked the pickup and got out. I followed him and watched as he monkeyed with the machine. First he put the transmission out of gear and adjusted the throttle. After that he opened the gas line over the carburetor, let it flow a couple of seconds, and shut it off. He took the crank from its place by the side of the engine and stuck it into the hole in the radiator guard. After a few cranks and pops, the engine started. Len reopened the gas flow, and the engine took off.

When it leveled out, Len said, "Go over and grab the tongue of that trailer, and we'll get hooked up. He pointed at a four-wheeled flatbed that turned on the front axle.

As I walked to the trailer, he went back to the pickup for a second. Then he got onto the tractor, put it in gear, cracked the throttle open, and pushed the hand clutch forward. The tractor took off, and he steered it in a wide circle around his pickup and in back of me until he came up alongside and passed me. He yanked the clutch, stopped the tractor with a skid, ground the transmission into reverse, cut the throttle, and backed up.

He stopped about six feet away and said, "Lift that tongue, and get ready to move it one way or another."

This was the kind of situation I didn't like. Someone like Len, who was always in a huff and a hurry, could back right over a guy in my spot, especially when the driver was looking over his shoulder and going backwards. If he was feathering the clutch back and forth, he might forget for a moment that the hand clutch on this old International worked the opposite from that of a John Deere or a Caterpillar, or he might just have his mind turned around, and at the second he thought he was disengaging the clutch, he could kick it in.

Except for one long-armed guy I knew, who just reached down from the low seat and hooked up by himself, this was the way everyone did it. Same with Len. He wanted to have a flunky standing in there. Feeling set up to get run over, I grabbed the tongue as I learned how, and when Len came wheeling back toward me, I jammed the tongue against the hitch and stayed ready to jump.

Len pulled the clutch as the metal clanged and the trailer jostled. He handed me the hitch pin as if he had eased up and barely touched the trailer tongue. I stuck the pin into the hole and banged down on it with my heel.

"Go ahead and get on," he said.

I climbed onto the trailer and stood in the middle as he opened the throttle again and took off. The girls in the cutting shed were little more than a blur, and then I kept my attention on the road ahead.

The Hubbs kids were sitting in the shade when we pulled up. Len told me to load the full boxes, and as I did, he told the kids to get all the ladders and buckets in order, and we'd be back in a while to load them up. It seemed to me that everything was already in one place, and he was just giving these kids a couple of hours of wages for sitting on their asses where no one could see them. I thought it might have something to do with Len being friendly with their mother. Remembering his comment about worthless people who were too drunk to come to work, I doubted that he was being nice to the sons on account of Hubbs himself.

At any rate, we left the kids there and went about picking up the boxes of fruit. At the drying yard we traded the full trailer for an empty one, then headed back to the orchard.

On the third trip we had less than half a load of full boxes and about forty empties. This time, Len put me to unloading.

I had time now to see the people who were cutting apricots. There were younger girls, from about twelve upwards, and there were grown-up women as well, some of them grey-haired, but I picked out a good half-dozen who were high-school age or older. They wore light-colored blouses, mostly sleeveless. Each girl had a ticket pinned to her blouse or shirt so that when she finished cutting a box of cots, she wouldn't have to wash the sticky stuff from her hands. The woman who looked like a warden came and punched the ticket. On some of the girls who caught my attention, the ticket fluttered on top of or next to a pook in the blouse, and it all looked calm and civil.

A water faucet ran in a constant flow, so that anyone who wanted to wash her hands could do it without gumming up the handle. For atmosphere, then, there was the trickle of water, the hum of voices, and music from the radio. The one song I remember hearing was "We'll Sing in the Sunshine," which if you listen to it isn't quite as breezy as it sounds.

Seeing those girls gave me a sense of longing, but I knew it did no good to wish for something a person couldn't have—things like a normal family such as other kids had, a cleaner house, a newer car, nicer clothes, or family vacations. A guy learned to do without, and even if it made him hard and cold, it kept him from being dissatisfied with his lot in life. In the case of these girls, I restrained my yearning. Like any young guy my age, I hoped to meet the right girl some day, but I knew I had to move up a notch first. Until then, the idea of what kind of a girl or what it might lead to was pretty dim.

Len showed up when I was finished unloading the trailer, and we went back to the orchard to get the ladders and buckets. The Hubbs kids were still loafing around, though it looked as if they had done about ten minutes' work to get the buckets in one place and the ladders standing in a group next to them.

Len cut the throttle and put the tractor out of gear. "Got 'em all?" he asked.

The older kid, Dean, said, "All except one bucket."

"What happened to it?"

Dean pointed at me. "He took it. It was my dad's bucket."

Len scowled. "What do you mean, he took it?"

"He put it in the trunk of his car."

I was caught off guard. I couldn't believe someone would tell such a pointless lie. As I was trying to think of what to say, Len turned his beady eyes at me.

"What's he talkin' about?"

"I don't know," I said. "It doesn't make any sense at all. You can look in my car, look in the trunk. I don't have any bucket."

Len gave me an irritated look. "We've got to have all the buckets," he said. "They get put away until next year. We use a different kind for pears. They got a canvas bottom that you unhook."

"Just count 'em," I said. "You know how many pickers you had."

"Well, they didn't all work on a ladder. When I say how many pickers I have, I count how many on ladders. The rest are just fractions. Like that fat kid."

"You can still count the buckets. Look, those young guys had four. Our bunch had six. These guys had three, and the Mexican family had four. That's seventeen. Three of them didn't work on ladders, or didn't have ladders to themselves, so there should be fourteen there."

"That's right," he said, quick and firm as if he was proving his point. "Now let's get this shit loaded up."

No one said any more about the bucket, but I don't know how anyone could keep from counting them after that. They all had to see that there were seventeen buckets and fourteen ladders, just like I said. We stacked everything on the trailer, rode back to the drying yard, and stored the stuff in a barn. All the time I was in the presence of that lying kid, I couldn't understand why he'd make up something so lame. I could understand that he didn't like me and wanted to get me in trouble, but I couldn't fathom why he tried it the way he did. After all, he'd had a couple of hours to think up a better lie than that, and if he couldn't, he could have at least hid the bucket.

As for Len, I could see why he put up with the kid. It would be for the same reason he gave the kids a couple of hours of wages. It he was going to get pissed at any of that bunch, it would be at Hubbs for staying home drunk and interrupting his social calls.

* * * * *

Late that afternoon, Len came by the labor camp with the checks. The four guys in the other half or our quonset were already cleaned up, packed, and ready to go. They had washed their red-and-white '58 Mercury and were leaning against it, chatting, as Mexican music drifted out of the open doors. As soon as Len gave them their checks they took off, driving slow but raising a trail of dust anyway.

The two swampers had already cleared out, but everyone else, as I understood it, was going to stay for the pears. I figured some more people would move in, not only in the two quonsets but in the house that had been empty all along.

For my part, I decided to stay on for a couple of reasons, even though I didn't like the foreman. For one thing, it always cost money to go to the next place and look for work, even if a guy didn't have to wait around for it to start. Here, I could sit tight and hang on to what little I had. The two front tires on my old De Soto were going bald and showing white cords, so if I stayed in the same place for another three weeks or so, I could get some better tires and still have something to travel on. I also admitted to myself that I was hoping to see more of Rosa María.

Chapter Six

In a stray moment it occurred to me that either of the empty houses—the one with the floor falling in or the one that Len was saving for a family—would have been a good hiding place for a bucket if the Hubbs kid had more ambition. I still resented him, and I was still irritated that I hadn't gotten any more satisfaction out of proving what an outright lie he had told, but I kept telling myself, like before, that it was better not to get into any trouble with him. So to make myself feel better, I thought about my good judgment.

I had come to think of myself as someone who tried to stay out of trouble. After being in and out of foster homes and working in one place and another, I learned I was better off by myself. When I avoided bad company, it was easier not to shoplift lunch meat or siphon gas. At some point after I turned eighteen, I realized a guy could get a record, and I didn't want that. But I also just didn't want trouble.

I remember one time when I was nineteen, traveling on my own. I was hitchhiking north, and I went where my rides took me. I got left off in Pismo Beach in the middle of the night. It was a small town, and there was no traffic on the highway. I walked out to the edge of town, carrying my bag, and stood in the cold fog. Across the way, in the dim glow of an overhead light, sat a service station with a couple of cars off to one side. After an hour of standing alone and letting the cold seep into me, I walked across the road. Both cars were backed in, so their noses pointed out toward me. One car was a Plymouth, '57 or so, and the other was a blue-green '55 Chevy. When I tried the doors, the back door of the Chevy opened, and I looked in at the dry back seat. I imagined crawling in, huddling up, and getting through the rest of the night that way. Then I imagined someone showing up in the morning and taking me for a vagrant. I closed the door, walked back across the road, and set out on foot. I left that town behind me and kept warm by walking along the edge of the highway.

From time to time I would think of that clammy night, and it would remind me of the way I ought to do things.

* * * * *

The labor camp didn't seem much different with the two back halves of the quonsets empty. The families across the road kept to their houses, Mack and Acie went over to A.D.'s as they often did, and I was left to a dinner of canned macaroni and cheese. I didn't mind eating by myself, but once I had the dishes washed, I felt a kind of emptiness setting in. Knowing that none of us was going to go to work the next day, or for a few days after that, gave me a sense of there not being enough order. Any of these other people, except for the Carrillos, could go on a drunk, and for my own part I would just as soon have something to do as well. I didn't see a few days off as any kind of a vacation.

After fidgeting around for a while I looked out the front window and saw Francisco and the two younger kids playing with the ball. Then I saw Rosa María on the doorstep, and I decided to go over and visit.

As I crossed the road, I waved to Francisco and called out in Spanish. I was glad Rosa María hadn't turned her back on me or gone into the house, so I walked towards her and said hello in English. She said hello and waited for me to speak again.

"Are you glad to be done with the apricots?" I asked.

"It doesn't matter. One thing is like another. We'll be picking something else pretty soon."

"I suppose. Your family's staying on for the pears, then?"

"That's what my father says."

"Well, that's good." When she didn't say anything, I added, "It always costs so much to go to the next place. And if you go somewhere to pick peaches, like these other guys did, it's ten degrees hotter there."

"So you're staying, too?"

"That's right. I think everyone who's still here is going to stay."

She gave a sulky look at the Hubbs house.

I said, "Yeah, I know. It wouldn't bother me if they left."

She let out a tired breath. "None of it lasts that long."

Neither of us said anything after that, and a couple of minutes later she excused herself and went into the house.

Dusk was falling, so I went back to my place and sat around. I was sorry my visit had ended so soon, but there wasn't much to do about it now. I was just restless. I looked out the side window and saw the lights on next door.

What the hell, I thought. I could visit with Mack and A.D. I didn't want to mooch their wine or beer, though, so I decided to go into Morgan Hill and get a six-pack. If I just went there and back, it would be all right.

* * * * *

The folks in the quonset next door had gotten a supply for themselves. Mack had a fifth of Ten High on the table next to A.D.'s gallon of muscatel, and Marge had a can of Pabst next to her pack of Raleighs. About a quarter of Mack's bottle was gone, so that was my clearest indication of how far along they were. The three of them seemed to be in a good mood as they invited me to sit down and join them. I had gotten a six-pack of Pabst in case Marge wanted one, but she was set up all right. As I took a can out for myself, A.D. told Steve to put the rest in the fridge.

I sat down, lit a cigarette, and opened my beer. I felt relaxed now. There was no one looking to start a fight or make up senseless lies, just some relaxed field workers doing what they were used to.

A.D. looked down at his Chesterfield through his glasses and said, "Mack and I were talking about the pears."

"Supposed to be four or five days away."

"That's what Len says. You know, they got to check the sugar content, stick those big needles in 'em."

"I haven't seen that."

"Yeah, they take samples." A.D. took a drag on his cigarette. "Anyway, it's about twenty miles down there, every

day. Mack and Acie are gonna ride with us. We were thinkin'
that if you wanted, you could ride with us, too. Save some
gas money, wear and tear on your car."

"That would be all right. I'd be glad to give you whatever's fair."

"We'll see what it comes to. It won't be much. I just
thought that if we were goin' down there anyway, you might
as well go along rather than drive by yourself. Unless you'd
rather do it that way, of course, which is your business."

"No, that's fine. I'll ride with the rest of you."

A.D. wrinkled his nose and re-set his glasses. "I didn't
think of this before, but maybe Harold wants you to ride with
him and his kids. That would be fair."

"I don't think they'll be inviting me," I said, "or if they
do, I don't think I'll take 'em up on it."

Mack rotated his whiskey glass as he looked up with his
yellowish eyes. "They give you some trouble?"

"The oldest kid tried to." I went on and told the story
about Dean and how he accused me of stealing the bucket. It
sounded as ridiculous when I told it as it did when it happened.

"That's the most dumb-ass think I've heard in a while,"
said Mack. "He must get it from his old man."

"Maybe," I said. "Harold seemed to think the Mexicans
were out to steal his buckets earlier. He told me he put a cigarette paper in the bottom of each one, and that kept the Mexicans from takin' 'em. I haven't figured that one out yet."

"Bah," said A.D., "that makes about as much sense as the kid saying you took the bucket, when they were all there to be counted."

I shook my head. "I just don't understand some people."

"Oh, yeah, you meet all kinds," said A.D. "People say things that no one could believe, and they act like it's normal. No sense of shame. Or they do things, just bare-faced as hell. I had a bunch steal our water jug one time in the prune orchard, and a couple of days later they ended up on the row next to us, and there they were, drinkin' out of our jug. I told Mike to ask 'em about it, and they said they had it all along. My ass. They'd been drinkin' out of a Clorox jug right up until they stole ours."

Mack spoke up. "That's the kind of shit you could expect from Hubbs. When someone goes on about everyone else trying to steal his stuff, chances are, he's got sticky fingers himself. Same goes for liars. They always assume everyone else is lyin', just because they do." He took a drink of whiskey, and after a wince he said, "That's what I tell Acie-Mack. You don't lie and you don't steal. Isn't that right, son?"

"Yes, Daddy."

"I don't care how flat-ass broke you get. You keep clean. Isn't that right, A.D.?"

"Oh, yeah. Ask my kids. You don't lie, you don't touch somethin' that's not yours, and you don't make trouble talkin' about other people. It's not that hard to keep to yourself."

Mack went on. "People know when you're talkin' out of your ass. Hell, no one's foolin' Len. He just puts up with it, and we won't say why." Mack turned to Acie. "Listen to

148

what A.D. says. Put that one on your list. Don't say shit that doesn't make sense."

Acie nodded. He was sitting on the couch between the other two kids, and they were playing some kind of a card game. When Acie looked at his cards again, his father got impatient.

"Did you hear what I said?"

"Yes, Daddy."

"What did I say?"

In a shaky, whimpering voice, Acie said, "To listen to A.D., and not say stuff."

"That's right. Don't be an asshole like Hubbs and his kids. I don't want to hear you talkin' shit."

"I won't."

Mack turned around in his seat. "Why in the hell would someone want to steal a pickin' bucket, anyway?"

A.D. pushed his glasses back. "Oh, they use 'em to wash dishes, or wash clothes or whatever, 'specially if they're camped somewhere that's not very well fixed up. That's why some outfits drill holes in the bottom, to keep people from walkin' off with 'em."

Mack looked at his whiskey glass. "I guess people'll steal anything. I saw it in the service, and a hunnerd places since then. Lie about anything, too. And talk shit."

Now Marge spoke up. "That's one think you can say for us. We might be broke, and we might get drunk, but we don't talk shit."

"That's why we get along so well," said Mack. "I don't either."

149

* * * * *

My feeling that order was starting to slip away began to get stronger the next day. Maybe part of it was that I didn't have anything to occupy myself, but part of it came from seeing how some of the other people pissed away their time and their money and whatever progress they were trying to make. That was assuming they were trying to make progress, and Rosa María had already made me wonder about that.

At a little after noon on the first day off, Hubbs went into town with his wife and kids and came back with a load of groceries. He was wearing a new white cowboy hat, the kind that's shellacked into a hard shell. He wore it cocked on the side of his head as he stood in the sun and directed his kids as they took in the groceries. After that he sat on the front porch with the hat tipped forward as he drank beer out of a blue can. I think it was Hamms. He drank one after another and smoked cigarettes right along. It looked like he was settling in on a real binge.

Mack and A.D. started drinking early that afternoon, too. Acie and the other two kids came over to get a pack of cigarettes for Mack, and when I asked the kids what they were doing, they said, nothing, just watching the grownups get drunk.

I was tempted to go get a six-pack myself, but I had just knocked one off the night before, and I made myself stay put. Every once in a while I got up and looked out the window, but I had the will power not to go anywhere.

At about mid-morning of the next day, I saw the green Oldsmobile come into the labor camp and park at the Hubbs shack. Fletcher and Bernie got out and went to the front porch. Blanche opened the door but didn't move from there, and after a few long minutes the two guys got into their car and backed around. As they drove out, they didn't glance my way. They were talking to each other, and they didn't look very happy.

Things got old by the middle of the day. A.D.'s kid Mike came over with Acie again, and he said Hubbs was on a real drunk now, lying in bed and hollering out at the rest. Mike said Fletcher and Bernie had come to get some money that Hubbs had borrowed from them a week earlier, but he was too drunk for Mrs. Hubbs to get a straight answer on how much he owed them, so she told them to come back in a day or two.

As for Mack and A.D., they weren't in such bad shape. Mike said they had finished off everything in the house the night before, and now they were getting ready to go into town to do the laundry. He helped Acie round up a pillow case of dirty clothes, and they went back to the other quonset.

A little while later, I heard A.D.'s Buick station wagon start up. I looked out and saw Mack getting in on the passenger's side. The yellow car backed out of its parking place in a half-turn, then straightened out and pulled away. I saw silhouettes of A.D. at the wheel, Marge in the middle, and Mack with his elbow sticking out the passenger's window. Mack sat taller than the other two, and his head looked large in the square cap he wore. I realized that wherever I saw him, Mack seemed to be just a little bit out of place. And now he was going to the laundromat.

Chapter Seven

I thought I heard a car come into the labor camp, but I kept myself from getting up and going to the window. I told myself I couldn't be jumping up at every little sound. I needed to relax and just let the time pass.

It wasn't easy, though. A.D.'s two kids came over with Acie and waited as Acie went into the room he shared with his father.

"He has to change his pants," said Mike.

"Oh." I had noticed more than once that Acie smelled like pee, so I just nodded.

A.D.'s kids were well-mannered, and I imagined that Acie didn't feel too embarrassed to hang around with them. After a few minutes he came out wearing dry pants, and the three kids went back to the other quonset.

A few minutes later I answered a knock on the door, and there stood Francisco. In his breathless Spanish he told me that the *señores* who sold things had come back.

I figured that was the car I heard, but it didn't interest me much. I told Francisco I didn't feel like buying anything.

"That doesn't matter," he said. "They're putting on a party."

"A party?"

"Yes, with sodas and beer and *pisto*."

Pisto was hard liquor, which didn't interest me either, but the idea of a beer was appealing. "Oh," I said.

"They are inviting you."

"Me?"

"Yes, and the young boys, too, if they want a soda."

"Do you want me to tell them?"

"Go ahead."

A few minutes later, I was headed for the party with the three kids trailing behind me. I could see the white 1960 Ford parked between the Hubbs house and the Carrillo house but a little farther in. I heard voices, and then I saw that the two families had hauled out tables and chairs and set them up in the shade of two oak trees. It was an old parking area where most of the gravel had been ground into the dirt, like the rutted road that ran through camp, but it was a level space and not littered with a bunch of junk.

Mrs. Hubbs and the two kids were seated near one table, while Mr. Carrillo, Francisco, and Rosa María were sitting on their side of the other table. The two vendors or bootleggers were sitting at the far end, more on the Carrillo side than on the Hubbs. A bottle of Old Crow sat on the table nearer to the Hubbs family but in a kind of no man's land, as it was not within anyone's reach and did not have the seal broken. In a square galvanized tub on the ground, about a dozen cans of Olympia sat on crushed ice, along with brown, blue, and green cans of Shasta soda.

The man who had tried to sell me a watch on the earlier visit called out in English and told us to help ourselves to the beer and soda.

I picked up a can of Olympia, opened it, and looked for a place to sit.

"Here," said Mrs. Hubbs, pointing at a chair between her and the hosts.

I went around and sat down, taking care not to look directly at Dean, though I saw he was smoking a cigarette and drinking a beer.

Mike and Steve and Acie all got sodas and sat on the ground near the Hubbs kids. The younger of the two, Ronnie, was smoking a cigarette.

Mrs. Hubbs had a neighborly tone as she said, "How are you today?"

"I'm all right," I said. "And yourself?"

"Good enough, I guess." She waved her head toward the house.

I nodded.

"He's having visions," she said.

I heard a murmur from the kids, and then in an exaggerated voice, Ronnie said, "Straighten out muh toes, Dean."

Dean himself gave a frown, as if he was too grown up to be making fun of his father.

Mrs. Hubbs spoke again. "Did Mack and A.D. go to town?"

"Yeah. Marge did, too."

She turned and spoke a couple of words to Dean, who shook out a cigarette from a pack of Viceroys. When she had it lit, she turned back to me and made a faint smile. I was sure she remembered the pack of cigarettes I had lent her, and I thought she was going to say something, but she didn't. She picked her can of Oly from the table in front of her and took a swig.

I shifted in my chair and nodded to the man on my right. He was not the one who had called out in English but the other one, who wore a turquoise ring and a gaudy watch band. I took him for the owner of the business or at least the one who had the larger share. I had gotten that impression before, and I had it now. He seemed sure of himself, sure of his control over the party they were putting on. On a small scale, he reeked of money.

He nodded at me, and I said, "*Buenas tardes.*"

"*Oh, hablas español,*" he said, and his face relaxed into a friendly smile.

He asked me my name, and when I told him, he held out his hand and said his name was Fidel.

I thought he was about as far as a person could get from Fidel Castro and still have that name and speak Spanish. Whereas the other Fidel was rugged and bearded in Army duds, this one was soft, clean-shaven with a trimmed mustache, and spreading out in a starched white shirt. He had a smooth, shiny face, with small dark eyes I remembered but couldn't see very well because of his sunglasses. Most people I had known who wore sunglasses either wanted to look like movie stars or had something to hide, like a hangover. He didn't seem quite like that, but he didn't seem like one of us, either. I saw him as the type who didn't do physical work but lived off of those who did. So he looked a little sleazy, but even if he was, I didn't think he was the kind who would do harm to someone or cheat someone—just opportunistic.

I shook out a cigarette, and his soft hand came forward with a chrome Ronson with the raised figure of a red rose on it. After he lit my cigarette, he took out his own pack of Winstons and lit one for himself.

He spoke to me, still in Spanish, asking me if I lived here by myself and worked alone.

I said yes.

That was all right, he said. It was good to work, but it was hard to get ahead. He knew that for himself. He had worked in the fields, but no one ever gave him a chance to do better. But that was the way things were, not anybody's fault.

He took a sip from his can of Olympia with the horseshoe on it. Oh, he had worked at a lot of things, he said. He had tried singing in the bars. He had his own taxi for a while. He was a labor contractor. Then he got into this business. It was good. He helped people have things they wanted, and he made enough to pay for his needs. Everyone had a right to try to make a living, get ahead.

All this time I could tell, like I did the first time I saw him, that he was making an effort not to look at Rosa María. He was paying plenty of attention to me, being casual and still being the generous host, motioning to Blanche Hubbs to have another beer and calling to the kids to make sure they all had sodas. Gradually I got a feel for the purpose of the party. Fidel and his pal had invited everybody in the camp, which gave the appearance at least that everyone was equally welcome, but I was convinced that Fidel was putting on the party to make a good impression on the girl.

He asked me about myself and what kind of work I had done. I ran through the list, which I knew pretty well in Spanish from all the conversations I had had in the fields.

Then he talked about himself some more. He liked people. He liked to go among them, meet different kinds of people, like me. He was glad to help people. Many times he had lost money by giving people credit, but he had helped them, just as he had helped the people who paid him in full. Thanks be to God, he had a good business. He did not want for anything. But a man wanted to be happy, not spend his whole life alone. He was sure I knew that. A man did not require a great deal from a girl, just someone who would look up to him and appreciate what he could give her, be proud of the life she would have with him.

As far as girls or women went, I had never spelled things out that clearly for myself. If I had, I know for sure that I wouldn't have spelled them out in those terms, but all the same, I could see where this fellow had his pride and in his way had earned it. He still seemed like a parasite to me, as well as kind of a would-be high-roller, but in spite of that I saw him as a real person with his real hopes and dreams. And I thought he was sincere in wanting us to drink his Olympia.

As I listened to him, the others at the party went on in their own ways—talking, moving around, getting a beer or soda, changing seats. The bottle of Old Crow went untouched. At some point Fidel's partner, Eleno, ended up sitting on the other side of Francisco's father, while Francisco took a seat on Fidel's right. When Fidel came to a stopping point in his conversation with me, he turned and spoke to Francisco. I didn't hear the words, but it seemed as if the man was asking the kid to do something. Francisco nodded and said, "*Oh, sí, sí.*"

Fidel reached into the pocket of his Frisco jeans and took out a wad of bills. I don't like to look at other people's money, so I turned away. A few seconds later, when I had let my head relax into its normal position, I saw Fidel tuck some folded bills into Francisco's shirt pocket. Fidel seemed matter-of-fact about it as he leaned back in his chair and stuffed the remaining bundle of money in his pocket.

The party flowed on. Blanche Hubbs went into the house for a few minutes, and while she was gone, her son Dean got a beer for each of them. As he set hers on the table in front of her chair, he did a good job of ignoring me. I noticed he had a faint blond mustache starting to grow, and he wore some kind of a medallion on a chain inside his t-shirt. On other occasions I had seen him with his cigarettes rolled up in his sleeve, but the t-shirt he was wearing had a pocket, so he carried his pack of Viceroys there.

He did not sit down as before but stayed on his feet, drifting for a few minutes and ending up not far from the tub where the beer was. He lit a cigarette and threw the match on the ground, then squared his shoulders and pushed out his chest. He had his head back and his nostrils showing, and he seemed to flex his muscle as he held his beer.

Blanche came back to her chair and sat down. After a minute she said, "You don't talk much."

"Oh, I just don't have much to say."

"Probably better that way. Seems like every time I say something, it's the wrong thing."

I didn't have anything to say to that. I didn't feel attracted to keep up the conversation, but I thought she was at least being neighborly. So I smiled and nodded, and she settled back in her chair with her new beer.

I looked around the party and saw that Francisco had gone to sit by his father again, while Eleno had fetched another dozen cans of soda and was putting them in the tub. Rosa María sat in her chair and gazed off across the yard in the direction of the orchards.

After Eleno sat down next to Fidel, the two younger Carrillo kids, the ones who liked to play with the soccer ball, went and helped themselves to more soda. Their father said something in Spanish to Francisco, who got up and went to look after the kids.

He came close to where Dean Hubbs was standing, and Dean tossed out a comment that I couldn't hear. Francisco straightened up and gave an angry look. Dean took a drag from his cigarette and blew the smoke out his nose. I thought he had a lot of cheek for a kid who wasn't eighteen yet, and he knew how to agitate someone. Francisco, who was about a year younger, was as quick to flare up as a fighting rooster. When Dean made another remark, Francisco jumped forward with his fists doubled.

Dean was taller and had longer arms, so he was able to shoot out his right hand, palm up, and glance it off the top of Francisco's head where his thick hair bushed forward.

Francisco staggered to the side, caught his balance, and came back swinging. This time Dean smacked him on the side of the head, then shoved and tripped him.

160

As Francisco got up and squared off, Ronnie, the younger Hubbs kid, came forward and said, "Let me fight him, Dean."

Dean lowered his fists. "He doesn't know how to fight."

Mr. Carrillo and Fidel were both calling out in Spanish, telling Francisco to let things go, but the kid shook his head and kept his fists up.

Ronnie was standing a couple of yards from Francisco. "Come on," he said.

I thought Blanche would say something, but she didn't.

The kid went on to say, "Fight me. Show your seester how brave you are." Then he spit, but it didn't go very far.

Francisco flew at the younger kid, and they starting pulling and shoving and punching. The scuffle went one way and another, and then the two of them went stumbling into the tables. The bottle of Old Crow fell over, thumped on the slanting table, slid, and broke open on the gravel.

Dean moved in, and I got up from my seat. I didn't know if he was going to try to get in some licks or if he was just helping his brother climb out of the spilled furniture.

Eleno had come around the table by now. He grabbed Francisco by one arm and yanked him away from the Hubbs kids. Eleno was a hard-looking guy, with his rough complexion and his tattooed arms, and he got things settled down.

Now that everyone was at a standoff, Blanche spoke out. "Damn it, Ronnie, you knock it off."

"Everybody's gonna knock it off," said Eleno. "We don't need no fightin' here."

Motion caught my eye, and I turned to see Rosa María go into the house. At that moment I also got a whiff of the spilled liquor.

Fidel waved his soft hand and said in English, "This is no good."

Things settled down some more. The Hubbs kids went into their house, and Francisco sat by his father again. After about a minute, he said something in Spanish.

"¿Cómo?" said his father.

Francisco rattled on, and I caught the basic meaning. The money Fidel had given him had fallen from his pocket.

"¿Cómo?" said his father again, in a tone that made the one word mean "How in the hell?"

"¿Qué pasó?" asked Fidel. What happened?

Francisco spoke across the space of six or eight feet. He said the money was gone.

A troubled look came onto Fidel's face. "What do you mean?" he asked, still in Spanish. "Did you drop it? Where is it?"

"It's been lost. It's not on the ground. I had it here in my pocket, and now it's gone." Francisco patted his shirt as he spoke with his hands.

"¿Cómo?" said his father. "What money?"

"The money this man gave me, to buy more sodas and beer if we needed. I was keeping it for him."

"How much is it?"

Francisco looked at Fidel. "How much?"

Fidel pushed out his lips, relaxed them, and said, "Some two hundred dollars."

I couldn't believe it. Actually, I could, but it seemed like poor judgment to give that much money to a kid to hang onto, just for the sake of looking like a roller. Two hundred dollars was a lot of money in a place like this, where most of us made twelve to fourteen dollars a day.

Now Francisco started rattling on about the two *chavalos*. He was waving his hand at their house.

Blanche caught some of the drift but not all of it, so she asked, "What's goin' on?"

Eleno explained that the gentleman had given the boy some money to keep, and the money had disappeared in the fight.

Blanche's face tightened. "Well, if you mean to say you think my two boys stole it—"

"I just say that the money is missing."

"This is no good," said Fidel in English. "We put the party, and someone take the money."

Mr. Carrillo called for Rosa María to come out. When she did, he asked her in English if she saw any money fall from Francisco's shirt or get picked up. She said no, she didn't see anything.

As she lingered with her hand on the door jamb, Fidel spoke again. "It don't matter. Maybe no one take the money. It just get lost." He shook his head. "No one gonna say some-one steal it. We got more money. We just forget it, have the party." He nodded. "Be friends."

Rosa María went into the house. Blanche got up and took her beer into her own house. Fidel waved his hand in a circular motion as he called to the Ashburn kids and Acie.

"Hey, you kids. You come an' sit at the table. Nobody gonna cause any trouble."

The party re-grouped, but there wasn't much to it. Francisco picked up the broken pieces of the Old Crow bottle, and the smell of whiskey thinned out. I kept my seat for a while. I wanted to be polite, and I didn't mind another beer, so I got myself one. But when that can of Oly was gone, I decided I didn't want to stick around just for the sake of drinking free beer. So I went back to my quonset.

There was still plenty of daylight left, and I felt I had nothing to do. This whole idea of sitting around waiting for the next crop had gone empty on me. I wondered if I should take off after all. I told myself I could decide tomorrow, not do anything rash.

I stretched out on the couch and closed my eyes. This was just a little mess, and it would blow over. But my God, give a kid two hundred dollars. Fidel ought to have his head examined.

Then I admitted to myself that I wouldn't have minded showing off if I had had the chance. I imagined knocking Dean Hubbs on his ass with Rosa María looking on. That was a nice thought, but I knew it was nothing more than the daydream of a guy killing time in a labor camp.

Chapter Eight

I was thinking of going into town to get a six-pack for myself when I heard a bunch of yelling and calling outside. I went to the front door to look out, and I saw Francisco and Eleno standing in the open area, facing the orchard. As they took turns calling out, I realized they were saying Fidel's name.

I went down the steps and walked along the ruts and gravel. When I asked Francisco what was going on, he told me in a rush of words that Fidel had gone to the bathroom and hadn't come back.

I asked where he went, and Francisco pointed in back of the quonsets and said he had gone to the outhouses.

Eleno added that *el señor*, meaning Señor Carrillo, had told Fidel to use the bathroom in the house but he didn't want to bother anyone, so he had gone to the rustic toilet.

I imagined fat and soft Fidel not wanting to walk past Rosa María to go to the bathroom, much less leave a smell in the house. It seemed a little comical, but I kept a straight face.

"He's been gone a long time," said Francisco.

"He wasn't drunk, was he?" I asked.

Eleno shook his head. "No, he drank just a couple of beers."

"Well, let's go look for him," I said, still in Spanish. I couldn't imagine Fidel snooping around in the two empty half-quonsets, but since I lived on that side of the camp, I didn't mind helping the other two peep in through a back door if we had to.

First, we went to the two outhouses, which were old wooden things with cracks in the weathered lumber. Both of them were unlocked and empty.

After that we looked into the two empty halves of the quonsets. I didn't expect to find him in there, as I didn't think he would have known they were empty. All the same I led the search, which didn't take long and didn't turn up anything.

We went outside again and started looking around the piles of pipe and old lumber. From there we went to a pump house, two rows into the orchard. I had seen it several times before and paid it very little attention, but as I saw it now, I realized Fidel might have mistaken it for an outhouse and then not had time to look anywhere else. There were weeds growing out a ways on all four sides, so for someone who had worked in the fields earlier in life and now found himself caught short, it was not the worst place to take cover.

We found him face-down in the dirt clods on the far side of the weathered pump house. His hat lay flipped on its side a few feet away, and his soft hands were spread out palm-down on either side. His turquoise ring and shiny watch looked out of place, but so did he in his sunglasses, clean white shirt, and black Frisco jeans. In another setting he might have been a tourist who fell out of the bus, or someone at an outdoor wedding who had taken a dizzy spell at the edge of the garden.

Eleno called his name, but the man on the ground didn't move. I saw Eleno's face tighten, and I knew he had seen trouble in his life. Rather than crouch or bend over, he used the toe of his boot to nudge his partner in the ribs. Then with the same foot he lifted the man's right arm and let it fall. Still frowning, he knelt and laid the back of his finger against Fidel's neck and then under his jaw.

Raising up but not looking at either Francisco or me, Eleno said, "*A lo mejor está muerto.*" He might be dead.

I looked at Francisco, and he looked at me. Then he said to Eleno, "What from?"

"I don't know. But he might have been hit on the head." Eleno looked at both of us. "This is no good. Not at all."

Francisco spoke in his usual rush. "We can try to help him. Take him back to the house, inside, where it's not so hot."

Eleno shook his head. "I don't think there's much use. And if something happened to him, we don't want to move him. The police are very special about that."

I nodded. I had never found a dead person before, but I knew that whenever there was trouble, you didn't touch it. You let the cops do that.

"I don't think there's a telephone in the camp," I said.

Eleno looked at Francisco and said, "I'll stay here. The two of you go and make the call." Still in Spanish, he said to me, "You have a car?"

"Yes, I do."

"Then go find a telephone. Probably in Morgan Hill." He pronounced it Mor-gawn Heel, like Francisco did, but I didn't find any charm in it at the moment.

"*Muy bien*," I said. Francisco and I set off at a fast walk, leaving Eleno to look after the body of his partner.

All the way into town and back, Francisco rattled on about the *chavalos*, the Hubbs kids, and how they had probably done this terrible thing. I thought it was pretty likely, but I didn't want to feed the fire, so I didn't say much. I also thought it had been stupid of Fidel to be flashing money and talking about how he had more, but if he was dead I didn't want to be saying something that would sound cold-hearted.

Besides, I knew that the Mexicans saw things in their own way, and since one of them might have been killed, it was not my place to be making light comments. I remembered one time, several years earlier, when I worked on a crew where there was a bunch of Mexican kids in the range of sixteen to nineteen. I was fifteen, and I got to be friends with them in the orchard. I jabbered with them and shared their jokes. One of them was a really dark guy with a broad, curved nose, and his pals all called him Cuervo, or Crow. The Mexicans have a lot of nicknames for one another, and they're not very squeamish about calling one another black or white or fat or whatever, so their calling this guy Cuervo seemed normal to me. Then one day I called him that, and he got pissed. He went on to tell me that he didn't make fun of me for the color of my skin or the color of my eyes, and how did I think he liked it? I remember his dark face and his angry eyes as he bored into me. I apologized, and I got along with him and the others for the rest of the time I worked with them.

So even if Fidel seemed kind of pompous, and unwise to boot, I didn't think it was my place to say it.

* * * * *

The cops hung around the labor camp through the latter part of the afternoon and on into the evening. They told everyone to stay in the camp until they were through with their questioning, and then they went from one house to the next. They came to my place last.

They were both deputy sheriffs, and they took the informal approach. They left their hats in the car and had a cheery tone as they came and went from the houses. The older one, Swanson, was light-haired and balding, while his partner, Coelho, had a full head of dark, short hair. They both chewed gum and carried note pads.

Swanson started by asking me what I knew of the incident. When I asked him what part he meant, he said, "The part in which the deceased, um, became deceased."

I said I was one of the three people who found the body.

"I understand that. I meant anything that happened or may have happened between the time he left the party and the time he was found."

I shook my head. "I left the party earlier. I was just hangin' around in here."

"By yourself?"

"Yeah."

"Do you live here alone?"

"No. One of the kids you saw next door lives here with his father. We live in this half, and the other half's empty right now."

"Uh-huh. But there was no one else here during that interval?"

"No. I was by myself."

"You didn't go out the back door, for example."

"No."

"But there's no one to testify that you were inside all that time."

I got irked at that. "No," I said, "and there's no one to testify that I went out, either, because I didn't."

"We're just trying to find out as much as we can."

It seemed to me that they were making insinuations as well, but I didn't say anything.

Coelho asked the next question. "How well did you know the deceased?"

I shrugged. "I had seen him once before, but I just met him today."

"What did you think of him?"

"Oh, I don't know. He was trying to be a nice guy, I guess."

"But you didn't like him."

"I didn't say that."

"Well, did you?"

I thought for a second. "I can't say that I liked him or disliked him, either one. He was puttin' on a show, but he was nice about it."

"You didn't mind drinking his beer."

"He practically insisted, but, no, I didn't."

Swanson came in again. "You know he had eyes for this Carrillo girl."

"He may have."

"Didn't that make you jealous?"

I frowned. "Not really. Why?"

Swanson scratched his thinning scalp. "Well, we heard that you had eyes for the girl, too, and you might not have liked someone coming in and throwing around some money to impress her."

"I can imagine where you heard that."

He gave me a matter-of-fact look. "We try to get as much information as we can."

"I don't know how much of that is information and how much is cheap talk."

"That's for us to decide."

I took a deliberate breath. "Well, even if I did resent the guy, which I didn't, it wouldn't be enough to make me want to do him in."

Swanson rubbed his nose back and forth as he looked down at his note pad. "There's the money angle, too, of course."

That burned me. "I make my own money," I said. "I don't scheme on anyone else's."

"Opportunities test a person."

"Look," I said, "you can search everything I've got, which isn't much. Search my car, search my room, search all my belongings." I took out my wallet and opened it. "That's all in Christ's world I've got."

He shrugged. "No one said you took his money. I just cited it as a possible motive. But as far as that's concerned, there's a thousand places where you could have stashed it."

"I suppose that should go for anyone else, then, too."

Coelho took his turn again. "Sure," he said. "Anyone who had both the motive and the opportunity."

I took a couple of seconds to let his comment sink in. Then I said, "So that makes me a suspect?"

"We're still at the stage of asking questions."

"Do you have any more to ask me?" I expected him to ask me who I thought had a motive and why, and whether I saw anything suspicious.

"Well, yes," he answered. "Do you plan to leave in the near future?"

"Leave? Like go somewhere else to work?"

He closed his eyes and opened them as he nodded.

"No, I'm not planning to go away."

"That would be just as well. Did you think I meant something else?"

"At some point I might want to go get a six-pack."

Coelho smiled. "There's no law against that. Just don't drink it in the car on the way back."

* * * * *

After the cops left, the hubbub started. Francisco came over and stood on my doorstep to tell me his side of the story. He said the cops had treated him as if he had been the one who clobbered Fidel. According to Francisco, the cops accused him of being too hot-tempered about protecting his sister's honor, and on top of that they said he was jealous of the man's money.

I asked him if he didn't have someone to account for where he was at the time of the attack, and he said he was gone for a little while. When I asked him what for, he said he was looking for the two hundred dollars he lost earlier. That sounded lame to me, until he told me he had been keeping an eye on the *gabachos*, which I interpreted to mean he had been spying on them. Even that sounded dumb, because if the Hubbs kids took it, which I thought they did, I doubted they were going to be flashing it around for someone like him to see. But I figured it seemed like a reasonable thing to do for a kid his age, frustrated by losing the money the way he did.

All the time he was telling me this, Blanche Hubbs was standing on her porch smoking a cigarette and giving an earful to Mike Ashburn. Dean and Ronnie, meanwhile, were carrying on a conversation with Steve and Acie. Mr. Carrillo was standing in front of his house taking it all in and making sure, I supposed, that his son didn't get into another fight with the *gabachos*.

It didn't take much to see that each of the two families was trying to get the rest of us to take sides. I imagined that before too long, either Blanche or Harold, if he sobered up, would give a try at convincing me that the Mexicans had caused all the trouble from beginning to end. I was just about to go back into the quonset and shut the door on the whole mess when A.D.'s Buick station wagon pulled in.

It looked as if Mack wasn't with them. Marge went right into the house, and A.D. called to Mike and Steve to come take in the groceries and laundry. As the boys did their work, A.D. told me a peculiar story.

For reasons he didn't state, but I assumed it was for the shopping, he and Marge and Mack had gone to San Jose. They found a laundromat, put the clothes in to wash, and went to a bar nearby to kill some time. After a while, A.D. and Marge went to put the clothes in the dryer, and Mack held their seats at the bar until they came back. The three of them had a few more drinks, then went to the laundromat again and folded the clothes. At that point Mack said he would just as soon stay at the bar while A.D. and Marge went grocery shopping, so they left him there and went to find a shopping center.

A couple of hours later, when they went back to the bar to pick up Mack, he wasn't there. A.D. asked the bartender what happened to the guy who had been with them earlier. That was where the story got strange, though A.D. was clear and pretty close to sober when he told it.

"The bartender said he left. I asked if he went by himself or with someone else, and the bartender said he didn't know. But before Mack took off, he left me a message. This is what the bartender says, anyway, but it doesn't make a damn bit of sense to me. According to him, Mack left a shell at the cash register. About this long and this big around." A.D. held his thumb and middle finger about six inches apart, then made a circle about an inch wide with his thumb and first finger.

"A shell?"

"Yeah, like a rifle shell, only bigger. Military."

"Oh."

"So Mack set this shell up on its end, on the side of the cash register, you know, on the ledge there, and told the bartender to give it to me, and I would know what it meant."

"What does it mean?"

"Hell if I know. Makes no sense at all. I wasn't in the service, and I couldn't tell you what kind of a gun that shell went in. I just know it's a hell of a lot bigger than anything I ever ran through a deer rifle."

"Do you have it?"

"I didn't touch the damn thing. I left it there."

"And no idea where Mack went."

"None at all. We looked all over that part of town. Went into every bar and restaurant. No one had seen him. No one knew a damn thing. I went back to the first bar and told the bartender we'd be back in the middle of the day tomorrow, so if Mack showed up, he could wait for us."

"That's a strange one."

"Sure as hell is. You can know someone like that, drink with him a few times, but you never know what goes through his head." A.D. glanced in the direction of the Hubbs shack. "Here comes his kid now. I guess we're gonna have to tell him his old man got lost. But he can stay at our place tonight."

"That's probably a good idea."

A.D. lit a cigarette there in the dusk and heaved out a cloud of smoke. "That's what you get for goin' somewhere. If we'd 've stayed home, nothing would have happened. That's what I tell the kids. You get a day off, you're better not goin' anywhere. But it's too late now. These kids behave themselves today?"

"As far as I know. But there was a little trouble here today."

The glow of his cigarette reflected in his eyeglasses. "Oh. What kind?"

"Quite a mess, actually. I'll tell you about it."

Chapter Nine

A.D. and Marge left in the Buick station wagon in the middle of the morning. As I stood at the side window of the hut and watched them go, I wondered how easy it would be to find someone like Mack if he was on a drunk. San Jose was a big place, and not everybody there was nice. I knew that much.

Left to myself, I pondered the mystery of Fidel losing his money and then getting knocked on the head for the rest of it. As for the first two hundred dollars, I was convinced that Dean had picked it up. The part I couldn't decide on was whether the kid had it in him to clobber a grown man and take money from his pocket. I thought Fletcher and Bernie were more capable of that kind of crime, except that they wouldn't do it for such a small return. Of course, they had left much earlier and weren't around anyway, and they wouldn't have known there was an opportunity. Dean, on the other hand, had to have seen Fidel's roll of money, and on his scale he might have thought it was a crime worth doing. Still, I couldn't decide whether he had it in him.

I mulled that over, off and on, as the next couple of hours dragged by. A sense of chaos and disorder, not to mention general restlessness, began to settle in on me. I guess it made some progress. At a little after noon I drove into Morgan Hill and bought a six-pack of Burgermeister.

Acie was still in the other quonset with the Ashburn kids, so I opened a can of Burgie and stood by the front window, thinking I might catch a glimpse of Rosa María. Within a few minutes, motion to the left caught my eye. The green Oldsmobile was coming into the camp. Like before, it rolled up to the Hubbs residence and came to a stop. Both guys got out, swaggering in their cutaway shirts, and stepped up onto the porch. Blanche opened the door, and after a few words she turned to her left, where the pale form of her husband appeared. A couple of minutes later, it looked as if something passed between the two parties, and then their voices rose in the way they do when a visit is ending. Fletcher and Bernie nodded their heads and walked back to their car.

The Oldsmobile rumbled, and a cloud of blue smoke came out. As the car went past my place, the two guys didn't glance my way, but I thought they looked satisfied.

Not long after that I heard the loud mufflers of the '56 Ford, and when I looked out I saw the two Hubbs kids leave the labor camp. A feeling of dislike welled up in me, so I went over and sat on the couch and tried to think about something else. Driving to town had given me a chance to worry about my worn tires again, and I got to thinking that maybe I should take care of them while I had the money and the time.

A knock came at the door. I figured it was Francisco again, so I didn't bother to put my beer away before I went to answer.

When I opened the door, I saw Blanche Hubbs standing there in one of her straight, sleeveless dresses that barely reached her knees. For a moment I thought she might have

178

come to repay the pack of cigarettes, but then I saw she was empty-handed.

"I heard about Mack," she said. "I hope they find him, for the boy's sake at least."

"Yeah, it's too bad."

She squinted in the sunlight. "I hate to ask you this, but can you loan me a cigarette?"

I shrugged. "Sure come on in. Get out of the sun." I went for my cigarettes and shook one out for her. When she took it, I lit a match and held it. She didn't seem to be in a hurry to leave, so I figured she was going to stay long enough to smoke the cigarette.

I didn't have any lights on, so the inside of the quonset hut was shadowy and felt kind of private. I asked her if she wanted a beer, and she said okay, so I got one for her and the two of us sat down on the couch.

She took a drink of her beer and huffed out a long breath of smoke. "Jesus," she said, "it's good to get away from that place, even if it's only for a minute. He drives me crazy when he gets drunk like that." She exhaled again. "The kids went to get more cigarettes. Thank God they can't buy beer for him." Then she motioned with her can of Burgie and said, "But this is good."

"Oh, it's all right."

When I finished my beer I asked her if she wanted another, and she said she'd take one. I brought it to her, then shook out a new cigarette for her. When I sat on the couch and leaned over to light it, she leaned toward me.

It happened before I could think about it. We each moved closer in the dim light. Then she had her hand on the back of my neck and held me to her, and we were locked in a long, wet kiss. It tasted like beer and cigarette smoke, but it drew me in. Within a minute we were both groping and shifting and pressing on the couch. A couple of minutes later she was on her back, drawing one leg out of her underwear, while I was sitting on the edge of the cushion, getting my pants down. Then I was on top of her, pushing into her, and it was as urgent and basic as something like that is going to be. Just as I was spending, I heard the mufflers of the Ford station wagon as it roared into the camp.

She said, "Oh, shit," and pulled her hips out from under me. She scooted back, swung around and sat up, and got her loose leg back into her underwear. As she stood up to get her dress straightened out, she said, "I've got to get the hell out of here."

"You can go out the back," I said. "Through the bathroom."

She lifted her cigarette from the ashtray where it had burned a long ash, and she took one drag before stubbing it out. Then she took a last swig of beer, patted her hair, and said, "Which way?"

I was pulling my pants on. I pointed and said, "There."

"O.K. Thanks." And she was gone.

I sat on the edge of the couch for a few minutes, catching my breath and gathering what wits I had. I was amazed at how everything seemed to happen by itself and then was over, as if it meant nothing at all. Maybe it didn't. I had had quick tumbles before and had felt empty afterwards, but I had never wished, as I did now, that I hadn't done it. I thought, here I was, the guy who had better judgment than to sleep in someone else's car, and then I pull a stunt like this one.

I got up, poured out the rest of her beer, and threw the empties in the trash. On top of everything else, now I had only two beers left. What a waste. Actually, this whole thing was a waste, sitting around waiting for the next job, and then getting caught up in a cheap situation and not doing any better than the rest of them. Morgan Cross, the man of caution, dumb enough to stick his dick in a knothole and wonder what was on the other side.

A knock sounded at the door, and I dreaded to go see who it was. But there was no way of pretending I wasn't home. I went to the door, opened it, and stood face-to-face with Dean Hubbs. He had his nostrils flared and his eyes in a tough-guy squint.

"What do you want?" I asked.

"Come outside, you prick."

"Oh, go away."

"Step outside. Are you chicken?"

"Sure, he's chicken," said his brother Ronnie. The kid was standing on the ground a few feet back.

"Chickenshit," said Dean.

"Just go away. Both of you."

"C'mon, c'mon," he said, each time giving a jerk to his head and a hooking motion with his index finger. "Unless you're afraid. Afraid to get whipped."

I could feel my blood rising, and I should have shut the door, but I didn't think I could when I was the one at fault. I stood there, silent for a moment.

He held his head up and back. "You just don't want to get whipped."

"Ah, go on."

"I'll go on," he said, and he grabbed at my t-shirt.

I batted his hand away, and he slapped me on the cheek with his left hand. That did it. I forgot he was a minor, and I just saw him as a smug trouble-maker who needed to be hit. If I made one mistake, I made two. One was punching him at all, and the other was not punching him sooner.

The fight was a mess, just like everything else. My first punch was not bad, as I leaned into it. But then he grabbed at my t-shirt again, and this time he caught it. He stretched the hell out of it and pulled me down the steps sideways as he stumbled backwards. I stayed on my feet as he lost his grip on my shirt and fell on all fours. I put up my fists and waited for him, and when he came up he threw dirt in my face. I had to step back for a second. When I did, he came at me, swinging wide with his right fist. It skidded off my cheekbone.

I squared off again, and he tried a maneuver that didn't fool me. He tossed his head up, faked a left jab, and tried to kick me in the nuts. I landed another right on the side of his head. He swung wide again and glanced his fist off my shoulder.

By now we had circled around, and I could see Harold Hubbs standing bareheaded in a white undershirt and a grey pair of pajama bottoms. He looked like the ghost of a lost hillbilly, and his voice sounded raw as he hollered out.

"Kick the son of a bitch! Kick the shit out of him!"

I circled some more, got the kid to cross his feet, and punched him a good one. Then his brother jumped on my back and grabbed me around the neck and head.

As I twisted to try to get him off, Dean came at me and slugged me twice on the side of the head. Ronnie was pulling at my face with his fingernails and trying to choke me with his other arm. I squirmed and shook until I got him to one side, and then I pushed him away. Meanwhile Dean was moving around, trying to get in position to hit me some more. When his brother fell off to the side, Dean rushed me and tried to tackle me to the ground. I got an arm wedged in and forced him back so that we were at a standstill. I thought I was doing all right until his brother blind-sided me with another attack, and then the three of us went down in the dirt.

Ronnie started biting my right arm, so I pulled it away and brought my elbow right back into his lip. That slowed him for a couple of seconds, but then I had to contend with Dean, who was trying to push one side of my head into the ground while he flailed punches on the other. I wrestled free and came up in a crouch. As Dean rushed me, I stood up and got my arms around him, lifted him, hoisted him on my hip, and tried to slam him to the ground. I didn't quite make it, though. He got his thumb on my throat, then jerked and thrashed and spilled away. As I let him go, something rolled out of his pants pocket and fell in the dirt. When I saw it I stopped, and so did he.

Lying in the dirt in the open area of the camp was a chrome Ronson lighter with the raised figure of a red rose on it.

"Well, by God," I said, "if that doesn't tell a story."

Dean rushed forward, stooping, and make a quick grab of it. "Fuck you," he said. "You don't know what you're talkin' about."

"I saw it," I said. "You can hide it or throw it away or do whatever you want, but I saw it. You and your brother both know I saw it."

"Fuck you," he said again, and the two of them took off at a fast walk to their house.

I looked around, and we had a pretty good audience. The Ashburn kids and Acie had come out to watch from the middle of the road, Blanche and Harold stood apart on their porch, and Francisco and Rosa María lingered in front of their house. I didn't know how many of them had seen the lighter itself, but I knew at least a few of them saw why the fight ended all at once. I don't think Harold recognized very much, because he was still carping to the kids about why they didn't finish the fight.

When the four of them had gone into the house, I turned and walked back to my quonset. I felt that everyone else's eyes were on me, and sooner or later they would hear some version of why the kids had come and picked the fight. The others might not know the last detail, but it would be enough for them to understand that I didn't keep my hands to myself.

Sure enough, about an hour later I heard from Francisco, who heard it from Mike Ashburn, that I had tried to make a pass at Mrs. Hubbs. I didn't ask Francisco if the story had reached his sister. I was too sick of the whole business to want to know.

Chapter Ten

There was no phone in the labor camp, so I don't know where the cops came from, but before long they showed up. Maybe Mr. Carrillo had gone to make a call without my noticing, or maybe the cops had just come back to follow up on their first visit. At any rate, they knocked on my door a few minutes after they arrived, and they said they'd like to ask me a few questions.

It was the same two as before, Swanson and Coelho, and they didn't seem so breezy this time. They came in and sat at the skimpy table and went to work on me. I was glad I had gotten cleaned up and changed clothes, but I knew they could tell I had been in some kind of a scuffle. I had seen myself in the mirror, and I felt their gaze on me. I had a scrape on the right side of my forehead, a bruise on my left cheekbone with fingernail scratches below it, and purple teeth marks on my right forearm.

The two deputies asked a lot more questions than they did the day before, and little by little they pumped everything out of me, including the first time Mrs. Hubbs had come to bum a cigarette, Dean's accusation that I had taken his father's bucket, my version of the fight that disrupted the party, how we found Fidel's body, what I did with Mrs. Hubbs, how the fight with Dean started, and how the whole thing ended when the lighter fell out. I had the distinct feeling that the cops would love to run me in for something, but at the end of their questioning they left me and went to talk to the Hubbs family.

A little while later I heard voices and a car door, and I looked out to see the cop car backing around. As it straightened out and took off, I saw Dean Hubbs sitting in the back seat.

Half an hour later, I heard another vehicle rumble in. It was Len the foreman in his pickup. He parked in front of the Hubbs shack, and Blanche came out and stood by his door for a long while. She smoked one cigarette and then another, which I imagined the kids had brought from town. Her voice went up and down as she bobbed her head, turned it aside to blow away smoke, and went on with her chatter.

I didn't like the feeling of hiding in my hut and peering through the window, and I had a hunch that some of what she was saying concerned me, so I went out and sat on my front step. She looked my way and seemed to squirm a little, and a few minutes later she went into the house, where I presumed her husband and younger son were holed up.

Len started his pickup, ground it into gear, turned it around, and put it in forward. I thought he was going to drive right past me, but he stopped and looked out at me. I went down the steps to see what he had to say.

"You need to pack your stuff and clear out."

"Me?"

"Yeah, you. You're done here."

"What for?"

He gave me his Richard Nixon scowl. "I can't have people startin' trouble."

As I took that in, I said, "Those kids came and picked the fight."

"I don't give a shit who started what. Usually if two guys get in a fight I fire 'em both, but I can't do that right now because I don't know what they're goin' to do with this kid, and I won't put a family out on the street."

I could see that arguing wasn't going to do any good. I let out a breath and said, "If that's the way you do things, then I guess I don't mind leaving."

He tapped the ash of his cigarette out the window. "I need to keep things in order here, or I won't get my fruit picked. And besides, I'm not sure you didn't have somethin' to do with those slickers losin' their two hundred dollars."

"Son of a bitch," I muttered. Things had changed quite a bit since Blanche had first hiked up her skirt, but it didn't surprise me.

"What?" said Len.

"Nothin'. Just talkin' to myself."

* * * * *

It didn't take me long to pack my stuff. As I was carrying the first of it out to my car, A.D. and Marge came rolling into the camp. I saw no sign of Mack. A.D. parked the car, and he and Marge sat there without opening a door. They didn't look like they were in a private conversation, just passing a bottle back and forth, so I went over to see what was new.

"Doesn't look like you found Mack."

"Nah." A.D. was wearing his glasses and his khaki cap as usual, and he looked weary as he leaned with his elbow on the steering wheel and took a slow drag on his cigarette.

"Any idea of where he might have gone?"

A.D. shook his head as he blew out the smoke. "None at all. We went back and looked all around, and not a damn thing. We couldn't stay around there forever, and the bartender was all for reporting it, so finally I told him to go ahead." A.D. took another drag. "I hate to talk to cops, much less put 'em on someone's trail, but I didn't know what else to do."

I nodded. "I guess Acie just stays with you for a while, then?"

"For a while. They said they'd send out someone from the county, and they'd keep him until they know more." A.D. breathed in and out with his mouth open. "It's the shits, but I don't know how I could have done any better."

"I sure don't know. I just asked because I'm takin' off, and I didn't think he could stay in this place alone."

"Oh, you decided to pull out, then, huh?"

"Len decided for me. I ended up gettin' in a fight with the Hubbs kid, so Len told me to clear out. There's more to it, but I don't feel like goin' into the whole thing."

"Hell with it." He held up the bottle, about the size of a fifth, with its green neck sticking out of a wrinkled brown bag.

"No, thanks."

"Well, there's other work. Just a pain in the ass to have to move."

"Doesn't amount to much."

"No, not really, when you come right down to it."

I went about loading up my things, and on my way in and out of the quonset I would get a glimpse of Mack and Acie's room. The door was open, and their belongings were strewn around on the floor. They didn't have much, and who knew what was going to become of it. I felt sorry for Acie, and worse, I thought it was just the kind of thing that happened to people like him and his dad. No right, no wrong—it just happened.

When I had my stuff in the car, there was one thing left to do. I went across the way and said good-bye to Francisco. He had seen me packing, and he knew why.

It was the *señora*, he said. She talked to the boss for a long time, trying to make everyone else look worse than her kids.

"It doesn't matter," I said. "It's done." I hesitated for a few seconds, and then I said, "Do you think I could say good-bye to your sister?"

"I'll go tell her."

She came out, clean and well combed, wearing a white blouse and a tan pair of jeans. "So you're going?" she asked, in English as usual.

"Yeah, the boss told me to pack up. It was for getting in the fight."

"That's too bad." She glanced at the other house. "Those people are a lot of trouble."

"Well, I got into some of it myself. I'm afraid I don't look very good."

She frowned as she gave me a once-over. "They didn't mark you up very bad."

I laughed. "No, I meant something else, but it doesn't matter."

Her eyebrows went up and down, and she said, "All of this passes."

"I guess so. I'm sorry to have to say good-bye, though."

"It's all right."

I hesitated, and then I said a line I had prepared. "If I'm ever in Eagle Pass, maybe I'll look you up."

She shrugged.

"Are you hard to find there?"

"We live on Mariposa Street."

Two minutes later, I was in my car and waiting for the engine to smooth out. I figured that wherever I went next, I would start over on my plan of moving up a notch. If I had left this place when the apricots were over, not stuck around for the pears, I could have been clear of the whole mess. But of course I had had my reasons for staying, not least among them my worn tires, and if I had left sooner, I might not have had that last conversation with Rosa María. I didn't know if I would see her again, but at least I had some dignity left, and some hope, as I drove away from the labor camp.

About the Author

John D. Nesbitt lives in the plains country of Wyoming, where he teaches English and Spanish at Eastern Wyoming College. His articles, reviews, fiction, and poetry have appeared in numerous magazines and anthologies. He has had more than thirty books published, including short story collections, contemporary novels, and traditional westerns, as well as textbooks for his courses. John has won many awards for his work, including two awards from the Wyoming State Historical Society (for fiction), two awards from Wyoming Writers for encouragement of other writers and service to the organization, two Wyoming Arts Council literary fellowships (one for fiction, one for non-fiction), a Will Rogers Medallion Award for *Dark Prairie* (a frontier mystery) and another for *Thorns on the Rose* (a poetry collection), a Western Writers of America Spur finalist award for his novel *Raven Springs*, and the Spur award itself for his short story "At the End of the Orchard" and for his novels *Trouble at the Redstone* and *Stranger in Thunder Basin*. His recent work includes *Poacher's Moon,* a contemporary novel; *Blue Horse Mesa,* a collection of western stories; and *Field Work,* a retro-noir fiction collection.. Visit his website at www.johndnesbitt.com

Watch for

Shadows on the Plain

by

John D. Nesbitt

"NESBITT IS A TRUE ARTIST."
—WESTERN AMERICAN LITERATURE

Visit us at www.speakingvolumes.us

A COLLECTION OF WESTERN STORIES

John D. Nesbitt

BLUE HORSE
M E S A

"NESBITT IS A TRUE ARTIST."
—WESTERN AMERICAN LITERATURE

Published by SpeakingVolumes

Visit us at www.speakingvolumes.us

Visit us at <u>www.speakingvolumes.us</u>

Visit us at <ins>www.speakingvolumes.us</ins>

John D. Nesbitt

LONESOME RANGE

RANGE

"NESBITT IS A TRUE ARTIST."
—WESTERN AMERICAN LITERATURE

Published by SpeakingVolumes

Visit us at www.speakingvolumes.us

"For the
Norden Boys
rings as true as a
triangle around
the chuckwagon
at suppertime."
—*True West*

FOR THE NORDEN BOYS

JOHN D. NESBITT

Visit us at www.speakingvolumes.us

Sign up for free and bargain books

Join the Speaking Volumes mailing list

Text

ILOVEBOOKS

to 22828 to get started.

Message and data rates may apply.